My House in Meuse

Gail Noble-Sanderson

Lavender Press   *Mount Vernon, WA*

Copyright © 2014 by Gail Noble-Sanderson

All rights reserved. No part of this book may be reproduced in any form or by any electronic or mechanical means, including information storage and retrieval systems, without permission in writing from the publisher, except by a reviewer, who may quote brief passages in a review. Scanning, uploading, and electronic distribution of this book or the facilitation of such without the permission of the publisher is prohibited. Please purchase only authorized electronic editions, and do not participate in or encourage electronic piracy of copyrighted materials. Your support of the author's rights is appreciated. Any member of educational institutions wishing to photocopy part of all of the work for classroom use, or anthology, should send inquiries to Lavender Press, Mount Vernon, WA

Printed in the United States of America
Library of Congress Cataloging-in-Publication Data

Noble-Sanderson, Gail
  My house in meuse / by Gail Noble-Sanderson
  ISBN: 9780615982250
  Library of Congress control number: 2014934967

Cover photo by Taya Sanderson Gray
Cover design by Rod Burton

Published and distributed by Lavender Press

This book is dedicated to all those who care for the wounded.

Acknowledgments

I deeply appreciate all of those who have provided their support, expertise and encouragement in this journey towards making this book a reality. Thank you to my editor and friend, Kelly Fisher. Your compassionate honest editing and amazing collaboration truly spurred this project forward! Thank you to my first early readers and dear friends Christine Genuit and Gale Frederick and my sister Kathleen Noble for their constant support and laughter. To our daughter, Taya Sanderson Gray, who read the initial draft of the manuscript and provided thoughtful insight into the flow and clarity of the story. Thank you to Ginger Nocera, a friend, fellow writer and SLP colleague, for your willingness to review my work as I once reviewed yours! How fun to collaborate! And to my dear friend Dominique Dailly who helped with all things French, and who is the soul of Solange.

And to Terry, my incredibly supportive husband. Your constant encouragement to "go for it" spurred me forward, and helped me remain true to the truth of my memories. I sincerely thank you all!

Prologue

They say a mother's love is powerful beyond what can be imagined. That it transcends all time. Losing you once Maman as you gave me life, I find you now as you give me life once again. Our memories, like love, transcend all time.

My House in Meuse

Chapter 1 – Growing up in Marseille, 1905 – 1915

Solange and I ran like the wind as it thrust us forward in bursts and fits. My large hood was secured with my free right hand, the other hand fiercely held by my sister. Finishing our marketing along the shops at the waterfront, we were caught completely unaware by this early spring mistral. Running, our filled market bags flew out sideways slapping themselves back against our chilled bodies as they caught the gusts of wind. My ankle-high boots were filling with water from above and below as the darkening sky dropped hail-drenched rain pelting our faces and lying heavy on our wool capes and hoods. Again and again the golden swords in the sky were accompanied by booms of sound!

"Solange, Solange! Look at the ships." I called over the wild noise of the wind.

They were bobbing and swaying up and down and side to side while sailors, also caught unaware by this sudden storm, frantically rushed to secure their decks. To my eight year old eyes, those men resembled nothing as much as little toy sailors on the little toy ships that I sometimes saw boys playing with (and wished I had some for myself). I wondered which ones were Papa's ships and Papa's sailors. I stopped and stared with a great desire to leap onboard and become a toy sailor myself. I could work on Papa's ships and be with him always on his travels.

My sister called out, "Marie, hurry! Stop your dawdling and stay up with me. We are soaked to the bone!" We ran another few minutes further along the waterfront before turning north onto our own *rue* toward home. Our house was constructed of a burnt red brick and attached to others very similar with only changes in the detailing. Two stories with tall wide windows front and back, the house was wide and square, solid and safe. Solange had us shake ourselves several times causing the wet to fly off our cloaks before opening the front door and stepping from the street into the foyer. She took our capes quickly to the kitchen to hang them on hooks by the stove to dry. I sat down on the foyer rug, untied my laces and released my feet from the wet leather. The carpet upon which I sat was splotched with water from our entrance, but still drier by far than most of myself. Solange told me it was woven in India. It was large, thick and multi-colored. Scooting on my bottom to find a dry spot, I leaned back against the solid front door and looked about our house.

The walls of the lower floor were paneled with dark luminous wood that forever smelled of wax and lemon polish. Those smells, mingled with the lingering scent of Papa's pipe tobacco, were to me the smells of home. The high ceilings were decorated round the tops of the walls by contrasting woods carved with lovely scrollwork and designs. My eyes moved along the familiar shapes identifying what I thought to be pinecones, leaves and perhaps a cluster of grapes here and there.

The foyer was broad and gleamed in marble of black and gray stone with sparks of red and silver and extended six meters both right and left and forward fifteen meters in front of me. To the right, the foyer led into the large sitting room with the dining area to its right. The highly polished wooden floors throughout the living areas were covered with the rich colors of carpets from foreign places. I stood up and looked into the sitting room where a welcoming fire blazed in the large stone hearth. The hearth stood centered in the room and occupied the focal point and place of gathering in our home. Tapestried divans and chairs with ottomans were placed semi-circled around the hearth, accompanied by a large low table set with cups for tea and a small plate of cakes. Smaller side tables stood beside other chairs and a small settee. This is where Solange and I spent much of our time reading, doing our needlework and stitching, and taking lessons from our tutors.

To the right of the sitting room was an expansive dining area with our long dark table already set for twelve for the evening's dinner. Papa's office was on the other side of the sitting room, and was separate and enclosed; his place of meeting and business when at home. Behind the hearth wall was the large kitchen, a substantial pantry, and several smaller rooms. Cook's own room was there as was another she used for laundry and storing of housekeeping supplies. A catch-all area, long and narrow, led out the rear door of the house into a small garden area where Cook tended her herbs and vegetables. We sat here often in the summer evenings, attempting to catch a breeze from the sea before retiring to the tight close heat of the bedrooms upstairs. More than once we found ourselves on such nights half asleep, laying on a blanket, identifying the constellations Papa so loved, and wondering if he was doing the same wherever he might be. The four bedrooms were all on the second floor and although Solange and I had separate rooms, we always slept together in hers. I often thought

Papa, when home, must have slept in his office as his bed seldom appeared ruffled.

Solange was six years my elder sister, and though we shared a common patronage our features must surely have resembled our own mothers', for Solange was as dark as I was fair. Dark and light; patient and impatient; brown eyed and blue; tall and taller. Solange and Marie. Solange had spent some time with both our mothers, and told me she had loved them both well. I glimpsed but one, only briefly and unremembered, my own dear Maman. She left us, passing in the night as I turned six days and Solange turned six years. Though as sisters we were opposites in so many ways, our voices claimed us as kin. Our deeper than typical-for-women contralto voices held the same deep timbre and were never more lovely than when Solange sang harmony to my melody. Try as I might, I could never accustom my ear to create Solange's lovely harmonies, so that was left to her. We loved to sing and Papa, when home, would often teach us snips of songs he picked up from foreign ports of call. He never seemed to remember all the words, and often it was obvious he would begin to make them up. When we pressed him to tell us all "the real words", he would laugh and tell us many of the songs were passed from sailor to sailor on the ships and not all quite fit for the ears of young ladies. We would merely improvise new words singing heartily and with gusto. Often at the endings of such a time of song, we three would sit very still with lingering smiles and tears of laughter in our eyes. Papa would slap both hands upon his thighs, and comment that nothing prepared a being for eating supper like a good round of singing.

Our love of music swirled round us as we sang and hummed through our days doing our fine stitching, cooking, and always walking from and about town. Solange would inevitably find a tune suitable for any event and most particularly for the townspeople we might cross paths with, as many were indeed our familiar acquaintances. She sang her opinions and comments rather than stating them in mere words. For Father Xavier and a party of mourners solemnly making their way to the cemetery - a snippet of a dirge. For Monsieur Cambrey stumbling across the stones and smelling of drink as he passed - a snatch of one of Papa's sailor songs. For a mother with a carefully tucked babe in arms - a Brahms's lullaby. And for Madame Dubrey, loudly scolding while tugging on the ears of her raucous twin boys, a bit of quick Mozart! Solange was at her most playful and witty during these times of musical observation, always acknowledged by me with a laugh, a sigh, or some sound that we both translated into mutual meaning. Music infused our lives illuminating even the most recurring and familiar events with a meaning particular to shared moments. We would hum Debussy while Cook lifted hot bread from the oven as we eagerly pulled off crusty bites filling our mouths while butter dripped down our lips. Only Debussy's eloquence could describe the indescribable.

During our very young years after my Maman passed, Papa attempted to install a series of "highly experienced" nannies, cooks and housekeepers. Solange was always a fierce and feisty youngster who approached each new caretaker as a threat and challenge to be conquered and tossed from our door. Solange of Exceptional

Fortitude (that was Papa's nom-de-plume for her as she pontificated a newly-devised plan of action against the current caregiver), connived ever more intolerable antics to convince every new nanny that they were never ever going to replace our Mamans and the only place they needed to fill was the doorway as they left our lives.

After a rather hasty exit by the fourth nanny within a year, Solange explained to Papa very formally, an attitude she carried off well, that neither she (now eight) nor I (now two) needed any nanny whatsoever. She was completely capable of taking care of the both of us. She told Papa that what we were in need of was a good cook and a full-time housekeeper because the present ones were inferior. She also wanted to discuss with Papa engaging tutors and, again of course, had a plan as to what we both needed in terms of beginning our schooling. Papa had always told us that when the time came for learning, our school would be at home. That suited Solange and what suited her suited me as well. Years later amidst laughter, Solange and Papa both agreed that the one nanny that outlasted the other three by at least two months seemed to have a had high tolerance for ear piercing screams, bites that scarred, and kicks resulting in shin bruises. Solange of Exceptional Fortitude!

She and I loved each other fiercely and togetherness was our constant. Papa, now at his wits end trying to run home and business and provide for these two young children, looked from one to the other of his small daring daughters. Solange had made this bold proposal for a no-nanny household after breakfast one morning where we appeared especially well groomed and turned out in fine dresses with our hair in braids as Papa preferred. Holding hands and looking up at Papa with expressions exuding confidence and postures straight, Papa relented to all of Solange's demands. He agreed to a six month trial of a no-nanny home with the other house staff replaced as soon as possible. Solange said she must be present during the interviews of cooks and housekeepers and together she and Papa would make the final decisions. And then they would need to begin to look for tutors as well.

Did Papa then smile at this bold, pragmatically feisty oldest daughter of his? Did he see the faithfully committed future aide-de-camp she was to become to him?

Solange and Papa were much alike. Indeed, he must have seen in her the same fierce determination to hold our small family tightly together by relying on our own strengths and unity. Although I knew only that she had, with great seriousness, instructed me to stand beside her, still and quiet, and to look only at Papa as she spoke to him of her plan, I knew as young as I was, that Solange had secured a victory for us that day and we could now look forward to peace in our home.

Over the next two weeks, Solange was indeed present when Papa interviewed a series of cooks and housekeepers. At the end of the final afternoon of applicants filing to and from our home, we all sat together as Papa and Solange decided which cook and housekeeper would begin to be part of our household. Solange told Papa that she wanted women who had kind eyes and ready smiles, for were we not to be a family?

And so Solange, at this young age of eight, began her career as domestic arbiter creating in our home a warm and comfortable atmosphere for the three of us. From her flowed a gift for employing and supporting all those who became part of our day-to-day experiences. She wove all of us together - cook, housekeeper, tutors and friends- tapping into each person's natural abilities to create a home that was full of wonderful smells, much laughter, engaging conversation, intellectual pursuits and a Papa who was secure and content in the knowledge that his own dear daughters were happy and thriving.

Solange's tutors became mine. Papa was fiercely protective and screened each one carefully. I am sure that in his circle of friends and acquaintances there were many who gave him names and references of tutors used by their own families. These teachers were always men; some young and some very old, some stuffy and others whimsical. Some smelled rather like mothballs, tobacco or old socks. Some had wit and ready smiles. Papa and Solange chose our teachers not only based on their education and knowledge in their particular areas of expertise, but on whether they would be good matches for what Papa called "our home education". Math, music, philosophy, languages and the arts were all exciting subjects of study, but my favorite was the study of history. History not only of past world events, but the way in which people had lived throughout time; how they thought about their world and each other. Religion also held a fascination for me as we practiced none ourselves. Most of our acquaintances were Catholic or Jewish and I looked with great curiosity and longing as we passed the churches and synagogues when walking to and from town. The study of history often intersected into the world of religion and I was an enthusiastic student of both.

As Papa travelled often and extensively, he had our teachers provide him with lists of what books, maps or other items they might require to augment our studies. Crates of books and treasures would arrive every few months and opening and unpacking all that Papa sent home from so many faraway places became for us our holidays. We spent long hours unpacking crates not only of books and maps but of beautiful gifts, artifacts and unexpected treasures. We knew even then, and spoke of it often as we grew older, that our education was exceptional and Papa our greatest teacher and advocate. We knew Papa despaired of leaving us so frequently at home for such long periods of time and the delivery of exotic items from exotic places somewhat assuaged his guilt. We did indeed appreciate these treasures! Papa chose well and over the years our home acquired small works of art which sat on tables and hung on walls sprinkled judiciously about our home. He was endlessly delighted to find them about when he returned from his travels. On his returns home, he would then tell us the story surrounding each acquisition. It was exciting and grand as each book and treasure always seemed surrounded by adventure! Papa's constant good nature and affection toward Solange and myself were the greatest gifts. To these we held fast and returned toward him one hundred fold.

Papa was a self-made man; widely read and more widely travelled. His places of study were the ports of Europe and the peoples of differing cultures he experienced when conducting his business. On his returns home, in the rare quiet evenings we infrequently spent alone with him, we could often pry from him exotic and exciting stories. He spoke several languages and because he could not write them as well as speak them, he insisted that Solange and I spoke and wrote equally well in Italian and English as well as our native French. We would often choose two days each week where we spoke only in a particular language. Italian was my favorite language; I dreamed of Italia. With Cook, we carefully prepared "language meals" for those two days of each week and she always joined us as we ate together teaching her phrases of Italian or English.

Papa also insisted we become "accomplished in domestic skills". Cook was much accomplished in the arts of needlework, embroidery and sewing and, along with cooking, taught us these skills as well. She became a great friend and *confidente* and we passed endless hours in the kitchen kneading and baking while she told us stories of her life growing up in a family of 12 siblings. She was the oldest and began cooking as she "took her first steps". When Papa was gone, we passed most winter evenings with her in the kitchen as we made meals and afterward worked on needlework often chatting late into the night. An endless source of hugs and witticisms, Cook was warm and loving and our great good matron.

As we grew older Solange began to assume more of the responsibilities of running the house, expanding and managing her domestic responsibilities with ease and enjoyment. Though she was efficient to the extreme and often intense in ensuring all the house was well organized and operating smoothly, she was ever calm and able to focus her intensity inward while mine was all focused outward.

Solange had a keen sense of propriety; always aware that we were extensions of others' perceptions of Papa. She constantly reminded me that our behavior and demeanor were closely observed in the markets of town, assessed at our ladies gatherings and volunteer events, and scrutinized by all who passed through our home. We were never more closely observed than when Papa hosted dinners with business associates around our dining table.

As young as twelve and together with Cook, Solange began to orchestrate Papa's business dinners and soirees. Solange and Papa would discuss who to invite, the seating arrangements and what would be prepared and served, including the wine to accompany each course. She demonstrated such astute insights, both culinary and social, as well as an innate political savviness, that after the first year of mutual planning Papa merely told her the date and who to include and she planned and executed, with ingenuity and grace, each dinner thereafter. Wines that were served were often grown by one in attendance, while another's caviar and olives were at the table, and still another's truffles. All felt welcomed and Solange and I were always aware of the keen sense of regard toward Papa as he bestowed upon each guest respect and acknowledgement. It was business, but refined business with the expectation that during dinner, all would be conducted with décor and good grace.

By the age of sixteen, Solange easily engaged in conversation with these men of commerce. Papa's associates came to relish an invitation to our home knowing the business would be conducted around excellent food and charming conversation. Solange sat at one end of the table and Papa at the other. I occasionally saw one of these businessmen cast an interested eye upon Solange in a way that had nothing to do with talk of shipping and commerce. I noticed that Papa saw it as well though Solange never seemed to notice, or chose not to. In our years in Marseille, I never knew Solange to show more than a polite interest in any of the men, young or old, that graced our table and our home.

I was always in attendance as well and sat at Papa's right side. His pride in his daughters was apparent. Being younger and at times not totally at ease, I did not often engage in the conversation. But ever considerate, Papa at some point in every dinner would place his hand round my back commenting to those at the table on my latest accomplishment in music or art; some comment to acknowledge and include me in the evening's conversation. I would squirm and fidget, eventually becoming bored by the conversation, but always I felt included and, taking cues from Solange, attempted to present my most lady-like self.

At the end of the several-course meal served and cleared by lady friends of Cook, the men retired to father's office to "get the business settled". The men would arise as one and move to the other side of the house into Papa's large study. There they would be offered cigars or tobacco for their pipes and Solange would offer brandy poured in cut crystal glasses from the cart waiting just inside Papa's study door. She and I would then go up to our rooms and go over every detail of that night's event. After an hour or so we began to hear cordial goodbyes and knew Papa would have concluded all the details for his next round of shipments. After the last gentlemen left, we would call down our goodnights to Papa and he would call them back up to us. Papa's business grew due as much to Solange's good efforts as to the growth in commerce brought on by a country standing in ready preparation at the edges of a coming conflict.

During these years, Papa often accompanied one of his ships to some foreign port. He was a man of action and hated being "cooped up on land". He said he felt "vital on the sea" and I envied him this freedom to come and go. And so he would leave us for two or more weeks, usually within a few days after one of the dinners. Solange would often instruct the housekeeper to only come but weekly and we would feel a sense of freedom as just she, Cook and myself filled our days as we chose.

When Papa was gone, we more frequently explored the ever expanding town attending concerts and readings. There was always the required presence of "other genteel ladies" as Papa described them to accompany us to all social gatherings and events. We would also reciprocate and invite friends into our home for tea or lunch which most often included a reading or music performance by an artist either local or passing through Marseille. I am sure that Solange paid them well and these, our own soirees, were much enjoyed by all and as Solange ever said, "increased Papa's esteem".

And thus many years flowed along. Solange, always constant, appeared happy and content. But as these years passed and the town around me became familiar in the extreme, the world and its unfolding events beckoned me to stretch beyond our predictable life. I became more and more restless.

Solange recognized the signs of my malcontent and made concerted attempts to keep me ever more busy and engaged. She added tutors and teachers and when I was approaching sixteen she employed a dance instructor. She even planned two small dance socials during that year when Papa was home. The furniture from our dining room was removed to become a ballroom floor and our house was filled with music and friends. I knew her intentions and understood both she and Papa's motives for wanting to keep me settled, but these activities in no way assuaged my restlessness.

During this time, Solange now required me to complete a list of responsibilities which she insisted she did not have the time to complete herself. I did them half-heartedly and not altogether well. These assignments to engage me were the result of my pulling away, and her compensating attempt to pull me back close. I continued to push away her encouragements to become more involved in the planning and arranging of Papa's formal business dinners. She prompted me also to put forth ideas and plans for excursions and activities that I might especially enjoy. I truly felt there was little left in Marseille that could prove interesting or fulfill this sense of increasing longing to move, and move beyond this place so secure and predictable.

I did not want to become an extension of my beloved sister. She found meaning and purpose in the life she had successfully created. She exuded a peaceful satisfaction with an existence I was beginning to find suffocating. Solange had created a life that well suited her talents, and I was ripping myself at my seams eager to create one that suited me half as well. Like Papa I had an intense need to feel "vital" – to move, explore and find myself caught up in places I knew nothing of but wanted to experience nonetheless. My desire to move outside and beyond my physical and emotional self caused sharp corners in my moods and more than once I cut Solange with my biting tongue.

    Perhaps my state of mind was more than youthful restlessness. Perhaps I reflected as well the uncertainty and changing of those times. The talk of possible turmoil and coming conflict made the edges of the days feel singed with worried anticipation. The climate all around us was restless and while people held fiercely secure to their predictable flow of months and years, the tides of change were approaching and I was poised to ride in its current.

Chapter 2 – Papa, 1913 – 1915

Papa was a barrel of a man. He was broad and round-chested set on thin legs. His thick chestnut hair rolled in waves across his head and extended his height to almost two meters. In the sun you saw the highlights of russet in those waves which were more predominant in his sideburns, moustache and beard. The years before the war brought tinges of gray as his business became more intense and the tensions of impending war were voiced ever more frequently in the conversations at dinnertime.

I did not want to think the graying of my Papa had anything to do with advancing age or worry. But I saw during those days leading up to conflict how his red-brown eyes, so like Solange's, reflected the strain brought on by overwork and tension. He was our rock – our world really, and though wearied with fatigue, he was always willing to tell us his stories and anecdotes of his travels. His adventures were our gateway into a broader, more exciting world.

Always over-heated, he wore as few layers of clothing as possible while still maintaining the dress of a gentleman of commerce. The heat within was mirrored by an exterior resembling either a roaring blaze of booming energy, or the carefully tended embers of dampened flames.

He would crackle and sparkle as he held court with his business comrades at our dinner fêtes, peppering the conversations with political opinions cloaked in sarcastic wry humor. With the exit of each dinner guest, he wound down a little more until it was just the three of us and he would once again become just our Papa. Our Papa was worldly, educated and wise, yet rooted deeply in all things practical. Commerce was his passion, his daughters and home his sanctuary to protect, and politics his religion.

When talk turned to shipping and trade routes, ships and cargo, his eyes would shine as dark jewels. Hands waving, thoughts flowing so quickly the words tumbled over themselves and not until his face was red did he remember to take a breath. "Innovation" was his message and he was an impassioned messenger for changing the "old ways of commerce". "Forward, forward!" was a term we often heard whether in regards to his business, our education, or the state of the world.

Solange always filled in the blanks of life attempting to answer my constant barrage of questions. What was it exactly Papa did in his business? Which were his ships? Where did they go? What did they carry?

When I was about twelve and began to ask these questions more frequently, Solange took me down to the harbor to show me Papa's fleet of ships. He had converted sailing vessels to steamers and these ships moved goods to and from ports up and down the coastline of France and more often now, as far north as the coast of Spain.

On our frequent trips to the markets, I would more likely than not attempt to engage Solange in conversation related to my desire to go exploring on Papa's ships.

"Look Solange," I said pointing to a ship just leaving the harbor, "do you not think that must be one of Papa's ships? I do think we are old enough for Papa to take us on an adventure soon. That would be so wonderful!"

"While it may sound very exciting Marie, Papa wants us to keep our feet firmly planted on the ground and leave the sea to him," she replied.

Moving down the lines of vessels to the market I asked, as I had multiple times, "Do you not think we could ask him just to take us on board and show us where he sleeps?" I persisted. "I would gladly ask him when we get home."

"You may ask Dear Sister, as you have at least two dozen times before, but until Papa is ready and willing, we will most likely not be walking the deck of a ship much less exploring its underbelly. We need to be patient Marie. Papa has promised that one day we will travel together to wherever we might want to go. I can hardly believe that might really happen."

And so our lives proceeded through those years of growing up in Marseille exemplified by routine and constancy. Papa built his business, Solange and I focused on our education and social past-times and when Papa was in port, our otherwise quiet home was filled with dinners and guests.

As the years moved forward the talk of politics and the possibility of war became more frequent. The topic of war now fueled the fires of conversation well beyond our polite dinner banter with Papa's guests. Papa would either be the most intensely loud or contribute the least to the verbose conversations regarding Germany and impending war. I often kept count of the number of glasses of wine each dinner guest consumed to determine if I could judge a correlation between wine consumption and a guest's escalating emotional outbursts that sometimes bordered on rage. It was then Papa would excuse Solange and myself from the table and we would slide up the stairs toward our rooms only to sit on the landing above listening to conversations we did not understand. Eventually the talk instilled in us both a deep sense of fear. When we became too sleepy or too frightened, or both, we would climb into Solange's bed and huddle together until sleep came. In the new day, Papa never referenced the talk at the table from the night before.

We began to see reflected in Papa's eyes his own fear as well as ours and his heightened sense of anxiety. We were all anxious in those days. Every person everywhere we went whispered the rumors of war and what it might mean. One woman friend paid us a call during a rare afternoon when Papa was at home. She began to expound over tea that it was "God's Truth" that war was "pulling at our bonnet strings and we needed to be prepared or we would lose our heads as well as our hats!" Papa soon thanked her for calling upon us and escorted her swiftly to the door.

Papa would often try and calm those that expressed agitation and fear. We all knew that the worry was based on more than rumors now. Fighting had begun and we did not know if or when it would come close to us. The fire within him burned quietly in those days of unrest and worried anticipation but never more than when someone would comment about "this Jew" or "that Jew" who was thinking of closing his tailoring business or his dry goods store. Papa's eyes would burn fiercely but he made no comment. These were men of business and commerce, well respected and successful, and counted among the many friends of Papa's. Solange, who handled all the details of Papa's business, told me of two such businessmen thinking of closing and leaving France. These men, she said, were also Papa's prime source for monetary transactions. I did not truly understand that significance, but knew only that it frightened me even more to think of friends contemplating the need to leave our country. Why and where would they go? Nothing made sense. Papa became quiet, absorbed, and the gray began to further invade his russet waves.

As 1914 approached, he also became more absent from home. His time was consumed by the increasing demands on shipping that readiness for war required. There were no more dinner parties, fewer social events and when Solange and I did go out it was just to market. We began to volunteer more frequently at functions the churches and Red Cross were sponsoring. When Papa was at home, men would come to see him singly or in pairs, meeting with him only behind the closed door of his study. Solange kept a cart just inside the door readied with brandy, clean glasses and sometimes a plate of savories. The glasses almost always gave evidence of having been used, but the food was seldom touched. Solange then simplified the tray's contents to include only clean glasses, drink and tobacco.

Only in those rare times at home now with just the three of us, would Papa's eyes soften and his voice become gentle as he shared with us his concerns. He would speak slowly; his voice pitched lower. It was as though each articulated sentence necessitated a singular focus to form speech from thoughts. We knew we could ask him any question and he would provide us with an answer he felt was honest and wise. We always felt safe, loved and worthy.

I was always more than a little curious about our religion – or lack of religion, as we practiced none. Most of our social acquaintances were Catholic and were always attending Mass on this or that Holy Day. Why did we not attend services of any kind? It was the topic I most dearly wanted to discuss with Papa. However the many times I attempted to approach the subject directly, he would only discuss religion from the perspective of our education and world history. But, I would argue, everyone had a culture; everyone came from some religion and I wanted to know more about ours. Early on in my inquiries, Solange told me we were Jewish. Her mother was Jewish, but she did not know if my Belgian-born mother was as well. It wasn't until much later in life that I came to understand the weight of significance Papa must surely have borne; perhaps wanting to educate us as to our heritage but, in not doing so, felt he was protecting us from possible future repercussions.

At those times when Papa waxed eloquent after two glasses of brandy, only then did I feel I could venture into questions of faith. One such evening with a few minutes alone with Papa I dared ask "Papa, if we are Jewish, why do we not go to Synagogue or observe Sabbath and Holy Days? I feel like we are hiding our history. Are we ashamed of our faith, or do you not believe in any religion at all?"

Sitting me down beside him with a serious intensity I had seldom seen in him, he told me, "Religion and heritage is a mantle placed on your wet head at birth. It is with you when you come in and will be with you when you leave."

"But Papa, our faith is rich in history and rituals. Why can we not celebrate who we are? It is confusing and I do wish you would give a concrete answer!" I replied, my voice had become somewhat intense.

"Marie, we do not need to perform rituals to know who we are, or for anyone with eyes to know who we are not. A wise man observes the rituals of others and keeps his own to himself," he replied with patience in his eyes.

Again I pushed, "I find it frustrating and certainly would like to at least enjoy a Sabbath with my Papa and Sister. Is that really too much to ask?"

"Yes, Marie, it is too much to ask! It is also unwise to even consider doing so. I know too well your frustration and felt much the same when I was younger. My Papa and Maman told me also to hold my countenance. Marie, explore your heritage within the confines of history. Study the ancient teachings, of all religions, and then hold yours in your heart as your own. We do not have to discuss this again my Dear. I only ask that you trust what I tell you."

As thankful as I was for Papa's words, I still had no sufficient answers to my questions. Sharing this conversation with Solange, she told me she had in the past asked Papa if we might celebrate Jewish customs and he had told her the same – adding that our home was visited by many but to be known by none. He forbid what he called "relics of faith" of any kind in the house.

We once asked if we could have a Rabbi tutor us in Judaic history and religion. He forbid that as well, saying Judaism was only to be studied in the context of history and world religions and our history tutor was certainly adequate to cover them all. Papa did sometimes quiz us regarding our understanding of Christianity, Buddhism, and Islam always ending with displaying our knowledge of Judaism. He would discuss with us the historical, social and economic influence of each religion and how world conflicts were rooted in religious ideologue. He would talk to us of how religions shaped the lands and peoples who embraced their faiths.

"And Judaism," I asked, "was there a country where it was the one religion practiced?"

Looking from Solange to myself he said, "Jews do not have a country but are a living mystery lived by its people in countries all over the world. Forty days was only the beginning as we have been strewn across the world and are wandering still." Solange and I had not heard him speak so personally of this mysterious faith of ours.

And then with a smile he said, "If we are God's chosen, He has a precarious way for them to live."

"But Papa, France is our home and our country!" I responded.

"Yes Child. France is our country but not our land. And we will not always be such free tenants".

I could not have known then how very wise our Papa was.

Chapter 3 – Nursing, July 1915

Three times a week, Solange and I walked to the Catholic Church close to the wharf. With each passing week, the Red Cross attempted to crowd together more tables and chairs to provide the ever growing numbers of volunteers a place to either sit or stand to cut, roll and stuff the empty boxes full of bandages to send off to the field hospitals.

The church's large grassy area facing the water accommodated all of the women in attendance more readily than the smaller rooms inside the church. Today however, the wind was whipping the soggy fabric of the tent wet from last night's storm, and the air was full of hot dampness.

The chatter was constant and caused me great agitation. The party atmosphere of the ladies dressed as though to go to tea felt disrespectful. Solange told me to "put my nose down"; that "my sensibilities were showing". Now 17 years of age, I had quite a well-developed sense of self-righteousness.

I had dressed in my house clothes adding a plain muslin apron over my house frock. Obviously I was serious about this work and felt my simple mode of dress appropriate for such. Solange was dressed down as well and, more due to the wind than decorum, we wore no hats but wound our hair in tight chignons to the back of our necks. I admit to a few silent giggles watching the ladies as they struggled to hold on to their hats while one-handedly rolling gauze with its flying white tail. Not an easy business, but a hat on one's head was at least as important as bandages in the box!

These thrice a week sessions added to my sense of frustration and restlessness. I wanted to bolt and run as soon as we would find a place at a table and begin the endless hours with gauze. Solange was a master of the polite conversation and would occasionally place a gentle hand on my knee as though calming a restless horse and, I knew, to encourage me to contribute an appropriate comment now and again. What would I do without her? She truly was my touchstone keeping me focused and steady while I attempted to find some meaning to it all.

The parish priest always hovered about moving table to table exclaiming what great work was being accomplished in God's name and today was no different. Red-faced and looking damp with a wheeze to his breathing, he was even more than his usually over-talkative blustering self. These volunteer efforts were officially organized by the Red Cross, and used the church's grounds only as a convenient locale to meet. The priest assumed that any activity on his sacred ground constituted solely the work of his church. He voiced great pride in "doing his part for our great soldiers". Not for the first time, I wondered what was involved in his "doing his part" as I never saw him roll a bandage or pack a box.

At the end of our second hour of work, the priest moved to the front of the tent and talking loudly over the sudden bursts of wind, introduced a Red Cross nurse who told us that this Friday she would be bringing a doctor to talk to us about training volunteers for nursing positions to fill the ever increasing need for helping with the wounded. Now I knew the cause for the Priest's over-excitement. I am sure he felt personally responsible for the Red Cross representative's upcoming visits. Again, it seemed, he was adding another notch to his growing godliness. I was certainly in a mood today.

We knew that the Red Cross was asking for the use of vacant buildings or spaces, even homes, which could be set up as hospitals to the north closer to the fighting yet some distance west of the front. Our group of volunteers had also discussed converting a vacant building here in town where returning wounded from our area could be nursed, cared for and hopefully rehabilitated. My ears perked up at the words "nurses' training"!

The Red Cross spokeswoman went on to ask us to "spread the news" regarding the meeting on Friday and to invite those that might be interested or have monies to donate to help with this effort of finding and training nurses. Someone asked if men could apply and were told that it was a good use of a man's time if he wasn't actively serving. We all knew men that were discouraged because they had not been accepted into the military. She said strong backs were needed as well as gentle hands. I would think a tolerance for blood and bewilderment was necessary as well. I knew I could do this. Nothing bothered my "sensibilities"!

I heard myself asking the nurse how long the meeting on Friday was to be; was it going to be held here on the lawn or inside the church? Did anyone have any more specifics regarding what the training entailed? Was the training weeks or months? Where was the training held? Where trainees would be sent? After listening to my long litany of questions, the nurse responded only that the meeting would begin at 10am, or "whenever the doctor arrived thereafter" and stated the meeting would not be longer than one hour and held in the meeting room in the basement of the church.

The priest was also pressed for information, but reiterated nothing more than what the nurse had already explained. They knew nothing more, but I wanted to know everything more! The nurse departed – on to the next town to continue recruiting efforts. We could only wait for the Friday's meeting and hope the doctor could provide answers to all questions.

The priest asked if any of us would be attending the meeting with the doctor, and if there were any among us that might see themselves as nurses. There were very few of us who were still unmarried or not attached in some way to jobs or other responsibilities. Many of the women had already taken jobs in the canneries, the local foundry or metal working factories. Their men were gone to the north, and the women were attempting to keep their families together, juggling caring for their children and working long hours at jobs suddenly made vacant by the town's lack of manpower. The conversation turned to worry about the children coming home to empty houses, and how thankful the mothers were to those with older children, and the older women willing to care for younger ones until their mothers returned home each day.

It seemed everyone but myself and Solange were engaged in working outside the home or helping tend other women's children.

Solange truly, as well as Papa, was engaged in work never ending and never more so than with the increasing commerce generated by the war machine. Solange increasingly spent her time completing documents arranging for shipment upon shipment as countries prepared for war. The massive amounts of paperwork needing to be completed was daunting and she worked long into the night, sometimes staying up late with Papa. He was now busy with overland shipments as well as those by sea. She had shared with me that she sometimes suspected many of Papa's services to France and the allies were clandestine, as he often asked her not to inquire as to what was being sent or the destination. These shipments went without official manifestos. Her constant support of Papa in these endeavors, the ongoing challenge of keeping him well fed and providing opportunities for less-than-adequate sleep for them both caused her to be busier than ever and ever more worried about it all. She became more quiet and reserved. Her liveliness receded as the work became more stressful and her resources flagged.

And there I was; restless and without purpose, seeking an experience both to satisfy myself and to provide assistance. Along with my restlessness, I felt a recurring sense of guilt. I was doing nothing more than rolling these white strips of cloth. I could do more. Something worthy, selfless, and so fatiguing that I would sleep soundly at night.

Our volunteer work was nearly finished for the day and as the priest turned to leave us, Solange attempted to catch my eye. I quickly looked away. But not so quickly that I did not catch the set of her jaw and her hands moving too quickly to roll the last of the gauze even more tightly. I knew her mind as well as she knew mine. She knew I was planning on attending the Friday meeting to hear what the doctor had to say. We were indeed going to have an interesting conversation on the way home. But I had made up my mind and would appease her by way of stating that I was merely interested in knowing what was involved; that I had no actual intentions of volunteering to be a nurse. I would assure her I would only listen and obtain information, but I knew she would not believe me, as I did not believe it myself.

Not even out to the street, she quickly turned to me, her voice in hushed but urgent tones, "Marie, you cannot – cannot, even play with the idea of becoming a nurse! It is dangerous and Papa would never ever relent to such a request!"

"Playing? You think I would be playing by considering this opportunity to do something useful? I would hope that you would esteem my abilities to make rational considerations and decisions in higher regard Dear Sister! I could do this you know! "

"Marie, it isn't a matter of whether you could or could not become a nurse. Of course you could! But the question is why would you? There is much you can do here without sacrificing your safety or well-being off in some dangerous place far from home. Papa will forbid it. You know that don't you?"

I stopped in the street placing my hand on her arm. "Solange, please look beyond your worries for me and Papa's concerns. Surely you know that I have not been altogether happy or at peace for some time now. Please tell me you understand! You know me better than anyone. Would you hold me back from attempting to find what it is I desire to do? Prevent me from becoming more than I am here? Tell me you understand and will help me!"

Before we turned to the front entrance of home, we had reached a compromise that I would go to the meeting on Friday and listen to the information the recruiting doctor provided. I would commit to nothing before talking with Solange further. She begged to go with me to the meeting, but I did not want to be distracted by the thoughts floating from her mind to mine. I wanted to be free to consider what might be.

And so I went alone that Friday at 10am and found twelve women already seated in the basement of the church's meeting room. Among them were those I did not know and women I knew by brief acquaintance from town, but none within our close social circle. None were here from our bandaging and boxing contingent. I silently harrumphed thinking that of course they would not be here. But word had obviously spread of the meeting today and I wondered what the intentions were of these other women. I discerned from scattered conversations that some were recent widows – both young and older and with no children. For the most part the women looked gaunt and tired. Some were disheveled of dress and hair. Others were ringing their hands and sitting in postures of isolation. Some were pulling at their skirts or picking at their lips. How could these women, who appeared distressed themselves, ever deal with nursing the sick and injured? Many though, also radiated a resolve I could not help but attribute to a possible need for retribution. Were they thinking volunteering could perhaps serve to atone for their losses or provide escape from pain? Where they patriotic or did they hold religious convictions that stirred their commitment to God or country? I did not know and admitted to myself that I saw them only as possible competitors for what I believed to be a limited number of training opportunities. My intentions were not as noble as what I perceived theirs to be. Did I want out of my present state of uselessness more than I wanted to specifically work as a nurse? Nursing would certainly make me useful and so with that, my one noble thought, I assuaged any guilt that might be lurking at the edges regarding my intentions. Truth was, I did want to help, to make a difference, and this seemed the perfect solution.

It was now past noon and still the doctor had not appeared. We were all fidgeting and restless, none more than me, and many needed to go to their jobs. Two women left for work but the rest remained in our seats. At 2:30pm the doctor finally arrived accompanied by a woman in nursing uniform. He was red in the face with sparse grey hair and accompanying pince-nez; his spectacles laid low on his nose and he appeared overly warm in his three piece tweed suit. He obviously knew he was far behind the scheduled time for his meeting with us. He did not apologize however, but quickly began speaking in short clipped phrases and without any seeming emotion or passion, said what he came to say.

He described the need for nurses both at the hospitals in existence and new hospitals being called into service across France. He also explained that some of the nurses finishing their training might be sent to field facilities closer to the front. These facilities moved as the fighting moved and posed danger from many sources not the least of which were Germans. He was moving up and down the country talking to women's groups to raise money for the hospitals and needed supplies as well as raising volunteers for the actual training.

He told us the Red Cross needed "women with a predisposed nature for nursing" which was "complementary of course to your gender's feminine and maternal instincts". He did not elaborate specifically with qualifying details and did not suffer many questions but turned the meeting over to the nurse accompanying him to explain the specifics of training. As he left quickly with a brisk step I wondered where he was off to next, where he doctored and had he been at the front and was he going back again? He somehow did not foster the notion of a man "predisposed with a nature" for doctoring in such harsh circumstances as war but I sensed he was very effective at raising money. Papa said wars ran on blood and money - the blood was hard to stop and the money hard to start.

All attention now turned to the nurse who remained. She was as tall as myself and appeared weary and solemn. I believed she knew firsthand about that which she spoke. She told us stories and gave examples of what we would face in the understaffed and underequipped hospitals and mobile battlefield sites. She also said that the men we would be taking care of presented serious injuries; limbs gone or just hanging by tendon or ligament, sight gone from chemical gassings, holes blown through their bodies, injuries to their heads both physical and mental and relentless fevers and often raging infections.

Some never spoke again before they passed, but for those that knew they were dying, we might also write letters for them to their loved ones. We would assist the doctors in whatever ways were needed including triage, dealing directly with the treatment of wounds and some nurses would work alongside physicians during surgeries. Taking on a look of absentness and as though the words found themselves spoken before she realized they came from her mouth , she said, "You live and breathe blood and death both awake and in your sleep. We can seldom wash away the red stains from our skin, much less from our uniforms. The sounds never leave your ears and the smells never leave your nose. Never in the history of war time has the need for nurses been this great, for never in the history of combat have there been weapons of war so cruel and devastating."

She painted a harsh reality as we all sat in rapt attention listening to what we might become on this possible journey toward such an ambition. She said some hospitals required more of nurses than others; some of the men would be injured to a greater degree and the doctors and more experienced nurses would provide additional training once we were assigned to a post. The initial training was two months after which time we would receive our initial nursing diploma. For the advanced level of Auxiliary Nurse, an additional six months of hospital experience was required.

"Oh yes," she went on to say as though an afterthought, "all training is paid for by the volunteer herself and there are no wages attached to your service thereafter. Therefore you must have some source of monies both to cover your training as well as your time in service. You will truly be volunteers, albeit trained volunteers, in every sense of the word." She paused and we resumed breathing. Four women stood and departed the room quietly and six of us remained. We were all still of movement examining within ourselves if we could possibility do what might be expected. She asked for questions and answered each one with patience and almost an air of relief that we hadn't all up and fled.

After we seemed to exhaust all possible questions and had again gone quiet, the nurse passed round forms we were to take and complete. If after a night of contemplation and talking with whomever we needed to talk with, we were still interested, had sufficient funds and wanted to volunteer, we would meet her the next day, Saturday morning at 9am back in this same room. Only those truly committed to moving forward to volunteer were to return as the timelines for leaving for training were short. Once we turned in our paperwork the next day, she would immediately conduct an exam with each volunteer, discusses the training schedules, and assign us a training site. We would then purchase our train tickets and travel north to the training hospitals in and about Paris.

One day to decide. If only Papa was traveling and out of town it would be so much easier. I knew Solange knew my heart and after terse and then tender conversations over the past days, she agreed to support my decision to volunteer. But facing Papa was a different story and I knew Solange dreaded it at least as much as I did. She would be blamed for my decision more than I.

Solange was waiting for me outside the church. As I paused in the doorway before walking down the steps to meet her, I saw her pacing back and forth, slowly wringing her hands in thought. She had been waiting all those hours. We went for tea at a nearby café and I told her all the doctor and nurse had to say. I knew I must present a face of strength to this commitment I did not altogether feel. My knees remained as weak as when I had arisen from my chair at the meeting's end. But still I held both her eyes and her hands as I pleaded with her to support me. My decision was made and I was going to do this.

After I had spoken all I had to say she loosened my hands, leaned back in the chair and looked round the café. Fighting the tears in her eyes from moving down her cheeks and brushing them away at the corners with her fingertips, she sat silent for many minutes. We were both taking time to compose ourselves before speaking further. I saw a softening in her dark eyes, and her face and body became lax with a decision made. She knew that she must either assist me in what ways she could, or break our bond of loving support. Over the years we often disagreed, but when one of us was sure about a thing with a great desire to see it accomplished, we were always there to support one another. This, however, was certainly a matter of considerable difference than a strong opinion about choosing tutors, dresses, or what our studies were to include. A different matter altogether. Would she support me now?

"Let me approach Papa first. You have no chance of winning favor if you storm in and make demands. This requires tact and diplomacy rather than a clash of two strong wills. I hate that you are putting me in this position Marie."

"I can be tactful when called for and I do not need to hide behind your skirts Solange! And in the end it doesn't matter how much Papa protests because I am going. And I am sorry that you even feel compelled to become involved in a matter in which I know you truly side with Papa."

"You do not completely understand my sentiments Marie. There is a part of me that wants to hug you and enthusiastically say, "Go, go!!" I do understand you and am proud of you for wanting to do this. But out of love for you and out of my own dread of personal pain for myself and Papa, I would never forgive myself if I agreed to such a thing and then it turned out horribly. Can you understand that Marie?"

"Yes, of course," I said exhaling all my held breath, "the last thing I desire is to inflect worry or pain upon you and Papa. You must know that as well. But do we sacrifice a life that could be better lived only to live a life lost – without meaning or risk?"

"Again Marie, let me talk to Papa first."

And so we left the café and made our way home walking arm in arm in silence and more slowly than usual, prolonging the meeting with Papa and gleaning strength from our tight hold on one another.

The truth was that I was relieved at Solange's offer to speak with Papa before I made my request, as I would likely demand that Papa acquiesce and state there was nothing he could do to stop me. Solange would be able to say the same but with finesse. I did want

Papa to understand; more than anything I wanted to be sent away with his blessing and not his wrath!

Once we were home and having shed our thin wraps (as slowly as possible I might add) we walked to Papa's study to find him still there. To my great chagrin he appeared not to have moved from his chair and his desk did not seem any tidier than when we left him hours earlier. His elbows were on the desktop with his large head cradled face down into his hands. This was not a good time. But I knew there would never truly be a good time. Solange and I exchanged a glance in acknowledgment of this fact and I held back just outside the door as Solange asked if she might enter and have a word. Pulling himself together, his posture now erect but his features still lined with unease and weariness, he quickly responded, "Of course my Dear. Come in. I am nearly finished here."

Solange pulled the door toward closing leaving enough open that I might stand outside, not quite seen but able to hear. She spoke slowly and quietly reminding Papa of our thrice weekly volunteer efforts with the Red Cross and rolling bandages and packing boxes of essentials for the soldiers. She told him about the announcement earlier in the week regarding seeking women to volunteer for nursing duties and that I was curious and had attended this meeting. The meeting had been earlier today and we had just returned home.

"Papa, Marie is of a mind that she is wanting to consider the opportunity to serve as a volunteer nurse. "

At this he sat up even straighter and it was obvious that Solange now had his undivided attention. "A nurse? Marie wants to become a nurse? What kind of a nurse?"

"Well Papa, I am sure you are aware that there is a great need for nurses to serve with the Red Cross. The Red Cross is here in Marseille this week seeking funding for hospitals, supplies and volunteers to be trained as nurses. They would provide the training and then the nurse would work in a hospital assisting in the treatment and care of the wounded. This is what Marie is considering."

His head dropped once again into his hands as we watched him struggle to compose himself. Without lifting his head he said, "Yes, I know of the need. I know of the training and I know of the risk. What I did not know was that such a thing was being considered within our family!"

I rounded the door walking in with as much confidence in my carriage and voice as I could command. "This would not be an act of family sedition Papa but fulfillment of a growing desire to move beyond what I have come to see as a stagnant life. I am restless and wanting more! Have you not seen that in me Papa? Can you not understand at all?"

"Yes. Yes, I have seen you growing discontent Marie and I know the restlessness. It is my companion as well." Pushing back his chair and hands pushing against the top of his desk, he slowly rose and walked over to the window.

"Do you feel a strong call toward nursing Marie?" he asked as I looked at his back.

"I don't know Papa, but I do feel a strong call to be away and to offer service. I am young, strong and I have little fear." I replied with strong resolution.

Without turning round, he said quietly, "When have you ever had to face fear Marie? My life has been devoted to assuring that you and Solange would never have cause to fear or doubt for your safety and well-being. And now you tell me you want to willingly place yourself in harm's way?" I could see his shoulders raising with a deeper timbre to his voice and saw the effort he was making to not allow the conversation to escalate to a place without reason.

"You know there is need at the train station also of volunteers in the canteen and even the infirmary. Would you not consider this Marie?" I saw the hope in his eyes as he turned round to face us, that maybe I had not considered this but would think it a viable alternative to my request.

"Papa, my heart's desire is to do this. I have the papers with me and I am asking, imploring you, to please sign them and allow me this freedom." I said as I pulled the papers from behind my skirts.

Looking now intensely into my eyes he said, "Freedom is a long road fraught on the way with hazards, temptations, and unexpected detours toward what we least expect. It seldom takes us where we thought we were going. Is this the journey you ask that I acquiesce to Marie?"

"Yes Papa. I am asking that when I leave it is knowing that you allow me to do so with the benefit of trusting me enough to use the good judgment I have learned from you. That you acknowledge, as

Solange and I do when you leave, that we always come home." Knowing he would attempt to persuade me otherwise, I had rehearsed these last sentences repeatedly in my head and delivered them with as much confidence as I could muster.

"If you were my son Marie, you would be off in the trenches and I would have naught to say about it. As it is, you are as spirited as any father might wish a son to be. Having daughters, I have always felt a deep sense of relief that I would never have to send a child of mine to war. And here I find again the best of plans thwarted by what I cannot control. Do you realize that the truth is you are incredibly naïve without any benefit of the realities of what awaits you?" He turned around toward the window once more and I could barely hear him say, "But then neither do our young men as we send them away with shouts of victory and acclaim their great valor."

After what seemed an interminable silence, he walked toward me and placed his big hands on my shoulders and with an audible sigh said, "I only ask Marie that you pledge to me you will keep safe and out of harm's way whenever you possibly have the choice. God knows I have lost too many women that I have loved and do not think I could bear it again."

Shaking me a little as though to truly sink this caution into my soul he asked, "Do you understand what I am saying Marie?"

I understood what he was saying. I would break his heart if I did not come home again as it would break ours if he ever did the same. "Yes Papa. I understand more than you could possibly know."

At that moment I only wanted to bury my head into his broad chest and relinquish all my plans, staying here safe and sound in our home in Marseille.

Chapter 4 – The Battles, Verdun, Apr. 1916 – Feb. 1917

I was sure my eyes were open, but I neither saw nor heard any sound. Nothing at all. Fearing I had died in the night from the shelling, I jumped from my cot. When my feet found the floor and I knew I was still alive, I grabbed my cape and flung open the tent flap.

The morning was shrouded in heavy damp fog. The smell of spent munitions hung heavy in the air. I knew I would always remember this odor of sulfur and fear. And blood, always the iron-tinged smell of blood I could never completely remove from myself. In what was now a constant habit, I rubbed my hands up and down, up and down, the front of my uniform. I had slept in my uniform again but had taken off the soiled apron and hung it across a stool. I would put a clean one on again before the day truly started. Looking at my almost clean hands and arms I knew I must have managed a quick washing before collapsing into sleep. Though constantly stained pink, my hands were free from the red stickiness. I must trim my nails again tonight I thought. Close trimming of my nails and brush scrubbing of my hands were the only way I ever hoped to remove all remnants of carnage.

I seldom remembered one day from another as the beginnings and endings and in-betweens were so similar; there was no sense of time passing. Only the constant passing of bodies between battle, triage and treatment. I ticked off in my head what I thought were yesterday's numbers. Twenty surgeries were not uncommon in a day, but I thought yesterday we had done more; twenty five at least.

The other nurses on my team, Jeanne and Annette, were already gone from our tent. It was still early and they had allowed me to sleep just a little later. The three of us worked every day side by side in the triage and surgery. We had trained together in Paris for nine months and left together for Verdun having been chosen to travel to the front as part of the surgical team for Dr. Claude Bisset. He had previously set up surgical teams like ours in other field hospitals and then returned to Paris to continue training others. When he put together our team, it was with the intent that this time he would remain with us as the Team's surgeon. We were posted to a field hospital west of Verdun some distance away from the trenches and the fighting. Jeanne, Annette and myself, as Dr. Bisset's nursing team, were often the recipients of both his praise and his frustration. We were dedicated to the doctor and our months of intense training in Paris had forged a tight bond of loyalty and friendship between us all. With so many surgeries in one day, such as yesterday's number, we were all on edge from the constant fatigue and continual frustration as we lost many men to the ravages of brutal wounds. Their limbs were often blown off their bodies, and bones shattered beyond salvaging. Amputations, though performed frequently and as quickly as possible, did not always result in salvation for the soldier who too frequently had other sites of severe injury to stave off death. Infection was the soldiers' other enemy as well. Yesterday had ended badly with Dr.

Bisset and other physicians taking their frustrations out on their nurses - again.

Before retiring for the night, my two colleagues and myself, in the semi-privacy of our tent, shared openly our own frustrations.

"I am sick of their ranting dismissals! Their arrogance is insufferable! How dare they even insinuate that today was made worse by any "inefficiencies" on our part?" I was furious and stormed around the tent rubbing my hands up and down my bloody apron front.

"Easy, easy Marie," calmed Annette. "It is only their fear."

"Well, we are all afraid and that is no excuse for their verbal attacks." I responded hotly.

"But they are afraid also of us," said Annette sitting heavily down onto her cot.

"Nurses? Doctors afraid of nurses?" I questioned.

"Not of nurses, of women. We are seeing our men, our heroes, naked, bleeding, screaming in agony and dying by the dozens. And the ones that are to snatch them from the precipice of death, our great doctors, are helpless in the face of such slaughter. Neither these soldiers nor our doctors were ever to be brought to such a place. Now, because they have been and are frightened beyond anything they could have imagined, they place their fear and humiliation upon us. They cannot bear it you see. But by our presence and forced calmness, we give evidence to their shame. The denigration of war has made frail minds of us all. But in the minds of men we have always been frail and therefore must be so now and blamed for their frailty as well."

I was stopped and stunned by Annette's explanation and sat down on my cot across from hers. "I think after this is all over Annette you must become a philosopher. Do you really think what you say can be true?"

"Oh most definitely! My father was a physician and when he lost patients or his treatments were not effective, my mother, brother and I always received the blunt end of his fear of incompetence. Many a late dinner time was passed with my father ranting about our laziness, our lack of ambition, our not being appreciative of how hard he worked, and on and on. We learned to keep quiet and eat quickly. This is no different. We must work as well as we can and hold our counsel."

"Keeping my counsel is not always easy for me! I wanted to throw a bloody limb across the table and hit them squarely in their heads," I countered.

"Well, remember that as women we have always been the weak ones; the gender to be sheltered and pitied. The ones needing care and nurturing. War has torn the mantle of masculinity from the heads of our men, and we reinforce their dependence on us as we work alongside them and bloody our hands in ways in which they believe were not meant for women. They all believe that women could not possibly cope with such horrific realities. I dream for the day after this is over that our service will be recognized; our role in working with the doctors at the front will result in opportunities beyond what we have now at home. We will have proven we are capable. For after this war, I am going to become a surgeon and take over my father's practice.

Won't he be surprised?" Annette finished this last thought with a smile across her lips as she lay down on her cot and went to sleep.

Throughout our training and our work together at the front, I had never heard Annette share such thoughts and ideas. But I knew that I agreed with her. We were not seen as equals, but as capable assistants at best and, at worst, necessary appendages providing a third, fourth or fifth hand to the doctor frantically attempting to stem the flow of blood, wipe clean the area needing to be cut into, removed, sown and bandaged. On most days, looking beyond fatigue, anger and frustration, I did know that Dr. Bisset respected our work with him. I held him in great esteem and wanted the same level of respect from him as well. I realized my anger was most likely my wanting his approval and lay at the heart of my unease at the end of such difficult days. I too hoped to continue my work once this nightmare ended. I had hopes of returning to the hospital in Paris continuing to work alongside Dr. Bisset in surgery. We had learned much in this field hospital of the dying and desperate. The need for quick action on the part of the medical team to save what lives we could, forced us, allowed us, to attempt in the moment between saving or losing a patient, extreme methods we would not have tried in the sterile surgical suites in the hospitals of Paris. I wanted something good to come from this mad surreal experience. Something I could take back and make sense of. Something that I could look my Papa in the eyes and say, "Yes, it was worth it, for I learned to be a better nurse. A better person. Someone who, in a saner world, can make a difference." And with that thought I too laid down on my cot and went to sleep.

The months proceeded in much the same vein. The shellings, gassings and trench fighting continued as daily we tended the never ending flow of wounded and dying men. Depending on the direction of the fighting, we sometimes moved our hospital site further to the west or the south. Ambulances and trucks arrived and we packed and loaded quickly and moved to a new field of operation. We were told in late November we would need to move once again. But the doctors, conferring with the military in command close to our site, decided the battle so wide spread around Verdun was waning. France was pushing back the Germans, the end was near and they felt it safe if we remained at our current location where it was determined we were most needed. Thus we stayed and triaged, treated and operated sending those seriously injured but deemed stable, to travel on the medical trains west to the hospitals in Paris. Those who were mortally wounded remained within our field hospital and we cared for them as best we could. Many died. Some of the soldiers recovered enough after treating their wounds or performing minor surgery that they returned directly to the trenches. Infection was rampant and I knew that many who returned to their stations of duty, if they survived another round of warfare, would ultimately die from infection.

In early December I woke up more disoriented than ever, not wanting to move and then realizing I was actually unable to move. My body felt hot and wet, the breeze drifting over me causing prickles of chills as sweat and blood dripped into my eyes, my nose, and my mouth.

The familiar and constant battlefield smells of sulfur, blood and feces washed through my nostrils more intense than usual. The sounds of moaning were close and punctuated by screams. I could do nothing but lay still with eyes closed and barely breathing. I willed myself calm and tried to take examination of my senses. Cold, it was so cold. I knew I was on the ground and that I was injured. I then remembered we had been shelled in the night and we ran from our tents as the fiery blasts hit close all around us.

I continued to be still, eyes clamped tightly closed dreading with every fiber of my being the condition in which I might find my body and the bodies of those that surely lay around me should I open my eyes. Maybe I was dying. Maybe I would die and be free of all this. With that thought I drifted off again from consciousness and time passed. Whether minutes or hours passed when I next awoke I couldn't know. I knew only it was night as I could see only dark through my closed lids. The night was full of low moans and the occasional sounds of weeping. I needed to open my eyes. I was thankful it was night time. Opening my eyes to a darkened reality might allow me to gradually return to a semblance of sanity. And I thought I could move.

In great pain I sat up and looked around in the complete darkness. Overcast and extremely cold, no stars illuminated the space around me. The darkness was a gift for which I cried grateful tears. Feeling no pain, I attempted to stand but found my legs not willing to assist in any manner as pain ripped through my body. My arms worked and functioned to help me to a sitting position but that lasted only a few minutes. Dizzy from the effort, I lay down on my back turning my head from side-to-side in an attempt to see what was left of us all and our makeshift hospital. I could see nothing. Even as my eyes adjusted to the dark, I saw no tents, no equipment, no one about to come and help. No one. The sound of my own weeping joined the chorus of the wounded I knew lay all around me. Some of us had survived. And with that thought, hung like a thin thread of hope around my heart, I drifted again into oblivion.

They said I fought well. I battled the infection that seeped into the wounds in my legs and travelled through my body bringing fevers and fits of chills. One leg was broken and both limbs torn open in deep wounds running the length of my calves. Thirty stitches in each leg. The broken leg was kept splinted not cast so the long site of stitches could heal more quickly. Severe concussion kept me in and out of reality for three weeks. During periods of wakefulness I spoke not a word. I had no thoughts, could formulate no questions and wanted only to go to sleep again. No one mentioned Dr. Bisset, Annette or Jeanne. If I did not ask, they would not be obliged to answer.

December through February was spent in the recovery ward of the hospital in Paris. I had been transported back to the same hospital in which I trained. My physical wounds were healing well and I was able to take short walks several times a day. I did so with the aide of crutches and the kind assistance from any one of the nurses. I was still speaking little, only one or two words at a time and perhaps only once or twice each day. I was continually told there would be no long-term consequences from the concussion and once I began speaking again, I would be well on my way to full recovery and able to travel home to Marseille.

In March of 1917, the doctor who had been assigned to my care, and did so with great compassion and diligence, came to pay me what he said was "a serious visit" to assess my readiness to return home. He said he felt there was no medical reason for my not speaking normally and requested that I try to speak. He said it was most important to my recovery that I speak openly and honestly about my condition and what I was feeling. Only then could he help me address my concerns. I did not think any of the staff realized I had "concerns". And what was this about my "condition"? I knew I had recovered from the concussion, knew that I was close to walking independently and knew that also meant shortly they would send me home - the place I did not want to go for I would be appearing on Papa's doorstep a wounded and broken person. I could not go home without a semblance of normalcy returned to my spirit as well as my body. Thoughts of Papa and Solange's concerned ministrations at seeing me come home impaired – defeated - were more grievous to me than any pain I now suffered.

With a huge sigh of resignation and some sense of relief, I began to talk. Where was Dr. Bisset, Jeanne and Annette? Were they alright? How many others were injured? How long had I been here, what month was it and had they contacted my family and could I please stay on and work in the hospital?

Gently the doctor disclosed that all three of my colleagues had been killed in the shelling. Twelve others died with them and many others who were injured that day had been here in the hospital. They had either recovered enough to be sent home or to places for long-term care. I was the only one injured from that day still remaining at the hospital. And, yes, my family knew I had been injured, that I was recovering and would soon be in contact with them regarding my plans for a homecoming. We would talk later about my remaining in Paris working in the hospital.

Shaking his finger at me with furrowed brow and stern voice, the doctor told me, "For the next two weeks Marie, you must do exactly as you are instructed. Eat what the nurses bring; and I mean all of it, exercise as much as possible walking around the ward and engage others in conversations. Come back to life Marie, and if at the end of the two weeks you can convince me you are able to begin nursing again, we will see what openings are available. Oh, and you must contact your sister and Papa within the next few days. They are very worried for you."

Without hesitation I quickly agreed to comply with each point promising that within the next two weeks I would be sufficiently recovered to begin my work again. I was overcome with grief at the loss of Dr. Bisset, Jeanne and Annette but betrayed nothing of my heavy heart to this physician who held my precarious future in his hands. I thanked him and bid him what I hoped was a hearty farewell and fell with a heavy heart back into my bed wrapping my sorrow round me tightly along with my blankets. Today I would grieve the loss of my friends and tomorrow I would begin again. I knew I could do this. I must do this, for otherwise I would be sent home.

Chapter 5 – Nursing in Paris, Mar. 1917 – Dec. 1919

The end of March found me standing alone on my own mended legs. Crutches gone, and with only a slight limp, I pleaded with my physician and the hospital's administration to allow me to resume my duties as a nurse. They knew me well; knew my determination, my skills, and I think they knew also that continuing my work was a way to continue my healing. They also knew I was not ready to go home. Two weeks into April I was cleared to return to part-time floor nursing. Both legs would ache by the end of my shortened shifts, but the pain was a paltry nuisance in exchange for remaining in Paris at the hospital with my fellow nurses and friends. I wrote to Papa and Solange of my continued gains toward full recovery as evidenced by having returned to my professional duties. This would reassure them, as it did me as well, that I would be whole again.

I remained at the hospital where I was most needed and during the next almost three years, the soldiers and their blood continued to flow through the surgical suites. In June of 1918, I returned to full-time shifts and I was placed first in surgical recovery where I tended the just-repaired-and-put-back-together. I found this easy work though somewhat tedious compared with what I was used to at the front where the pace was furious and there was little time to think of anything but the injured in front of you. Soon I was requesting to assist in surgery. There was constant turnover of nurses coming and going and I reminded my supervisors again and again of my field experience. They assured me they didn't need to be reminded. They knew I possessed the skills, but what none of us was sure of was whether I was emotionally ready to return to the intensity and pace of participating in surgeries. By the end of July, after much convincing to both myself and others, I secured the night surgery shift. I approached that first night back in surgery with great anticipation pushing aside any hesitation I might have felt as to whether I was prepared for what was always the theatre of the unexpected.

Halfway through the amputation the sweating and dizziness began. I heard voices; people shouting, screams inside my head and felt an overwhelming urgency to run. Run as quickly as possible away from the blood and the screams before I vomited or fainted – or both. I was escorted from the surgery suite. Another nurse took me to the recovery area where I had spent so much time tending those in similar distress. As my breathing slowed my feelings of panic ebbed as well. Mon Dieu! I was so embarrassed. I felt so ashamed, humiliated and felt such a sense of failure that at that moment I wanted nothing more than to be anywhere else than at my beloved hospital. A nurse that could not nurse! A woman who could not pull herself together to do what she had been trained to do and had done so well. Before that is; before this place my mind went to of its own accord. A place I knew I was still running from. How would I escape and return? I felt I was going insane.

The next seven days I spent in my room in the nursing dormitory and only left for meals and scheduled appointments with a physician on staff who spent thirty minutes each day talking with me about my panic in the surgery suite My flashbacks of memory were not really specific individual memories, but a compilation of the horrible sights and sounds I had experienced all exploding in my head. I came to realize that my need to remain constantly busy, even hectic and overly fatigued, stemmed from my fear that those moments of panic lay close to the surface waiting only to be spilled to overflowing by a trigger that might catch me unaware. Long work hours, consistent routine, and constant fatigue was the dam keeping the panic contained.

My compassionate physician-counselor explained that many serving on the fields of battle came home with what the medical profession was calling *neurasthenie* or "neurasthenia". I later learned this emotional state was more commonly referred to as *une crise de tristesse sombre*: "a crisis of black melancholy". He assured me there was no need for shame, but that I needed to be patient with myself and allow my mind and spirit time to continue healing. He assured me that with time I would no longer feel the panic and fear nor the utter despair that occasionally came over me as well. After a week of like discussions, I told the physician I would understand if they would want me to give up my position at the hospital and return to Marseille.

"On the contrary Marie," the doctor said as he sat back in his chair and looked at me thoughtfully, "we were hoping that you would consider two positions here. Part of your hours in the surgery suite only when the doctor is ready to close the patient's wound site and your remaining time working in the ward where the men are suffering similar concerns as yours but to a much greater degree. Your patients would then benefit by both your nursing skills and your understanding of these secondary after-effects of battle."

"While I am very appreciative of this offer, I will need a few days' time to consider if I am capable of what you are asking," I responded. I was still so shaken from what had occurred in the surgery suite that I was not sure I could return there under any circumstances. And I was certainly unsure as to whether I desired to attend patients who would remind me every day of my own battles. What if it happened again when in surgery or made my own situation worse by attempting to care for those "suffering similar concerns" as the doctor had put it?

"Give it some thought Marie. Let's first continue to meet each day this next week. I think you will find by discussing and facing your fears you might eventually lay them to rest. After this next week, think about returning again to your position in surgical recovery only. Gradually, as you feel you are able, you might begin just to enter the surgery suite as an observer and then gradually, depending on those results, eventually assist the physicians once again with closings. You must decide what it is you most want to do and then together we can move forward. All must be gradual but all can be achieved with patience and courage. I know that you have both." With that he stood, took my elbow and ushered me to the door. I pensively returned to my room.

Why would the physicians still want me to participate in any aspect of surgery, let alone in closing a patient's surgery site after my display of panic? I knew it was because of my stitching. My years of needlework with Solange pulling thread in and out of light and heavy material in rows of small precise tight stitches proved of great benefit to the completion of a successful surgery. I had a gift for suturing. I could sew a wound or surgery site together with great speed, greater accuracy and in neat stitches that left only a small straight scar. And because of my strict and consistent practice of sterilizing everything that came in contact with the patient, those I put back together seldom had secondary infections at the surgery site. I was in great demand in the surgery suites.

Gradually I did re-enter the surgery suite, but only at the end of a procedure when my sewing skills were needed. I resumed my work in surgical recovery and would, on most days, be called into the surgery suite once or twice each shift to assist in closing. However, I did not acquiesce to working in the sanatorium ward. I convinced myself it was too far a physical distance from the surgery ward where I might be needed at short notice. It was much more efficient if I remained working in surgical recovery where I could move in and out of surgery quickly as needed. My physician-counselor seemed to understand my reticence and did not argue with my logic regarding efficiency. He did request that we continue to meet one hour a week. We did and I found I both dreaded and anticipated those sessions of talk. During our conversations my pain would rise up to the surface where it had to be acknowledged and occasionally, catching me surprised and relieved, it seemed to rise above and out of me. It seemed unending; this acknowledgment and purging of the past. The doctor was encouraging, saying I was doing well, and that eventually the painful memories would be completely dispelled and I would be free. I chose to believe him and strived to recount and release what came into my mind. Once I was empty, I believed, it would be over.

There were many other nurses and physicians at the hospital who had also worked at the front in various field hospitals close to battle sites. We formed a close-knit community and spent most of our off hours together walking Paris and taking our meals in small cafés about the city. We did not spend our time re-living the past but talked only of the present and more about the future. We were all wanting to move forward but were holding fast to the security the hospital work provided us both in terms of our careers as well as a familiar and safe environment in which to think about what we might do when the world was sane again.

The lively, often intense conversations with my close nursing friends would move from the hilarious to the more serious as we spoke with excitement about the future of modern medicine, equality and the eventual vote for women, what we wanted to do, where we would live and where we might travel. We never spoke of who we might love or when we would actually be going back to our families.

Though often difficult to put pen to paper, I faithfully wrote to Solange and Papa several times a week. Solange's letters and mine flew with regularity between Paris and Marseille. After a time she stopped asking when I might be coming home. Stopped telling me about the openings at the hospital in Marseille where I could "easily find work" and just began to fill her letters with anecdotes from home. I had shared only vague brushstrokes of what my journey had been regarding both my physical and emotional recovery and I appreciated her patience as I continued to be patient with myself. Eventually I returned to where I truly felt I belonged as a nurse – in the surgery suites assisting the doctors. I kept the memories and the feelings of despair and panic pushed back deep into the recesses of my mind. I did my job and did it well and thought myself quite repaired.

I always knew I would be returning to Marseille, but knew also that it must be in my own time when I felt I was prepared to face those I had not seen for several years and for them to perhaps prepare to face a grown and changed Marie. Someone they might not know as well as they assumed. Someone different.

At the beginning of December 1919, feeling fully recovered and therefore with some semblance of returned confidence, I submitted my resignation to the hospital and began packing my trunk. I wrote Solange and Papa to expect me home by the end of December. The mailing of this letter was accompanied by feelings of great homesickness as well as great fear.

I had carried my nursing diploma to the front with me and it was lost along with so many other things I had held dear. On my last day before leaving, my friends, fellow nurses, and even many of the physicians, surprised me with a final fête and awarded me a new diploma to replace the one lost at the front. The diploma they presented to me was that of an Advanced Auxiliary Nurse stating in an attached letter signed by the hospital's supervising physician, a summary of the history of my training beginning at this same hospital in 1915, my service during the war in the field hospitals, and my work and additional training here again in Paris. My feelings of appreciation were beyond my ability to express in mere words. They were dear friends and exceptional colleagues.

A military representative also in attendance at my going away, presented me with a pin he attached to my uniform as acknowledgement of my service to France as a Red Cross Nurse and specifically my service during the Battle of Verdun. Once again I was speechless and much pleased. At that moment I felt all was well, all was healed. I knew Papa would be proud of me.

To say that it was difficult to leave Paris would be untrue. To say that it was difficult to leave the hospital, my friends and my patients, was an understatement. With many hugs and tears I boarded the train mid-afternoon in late December, the snow falling heavily on my dark nurse's cloak. I was wearing my uniform home with my accomplishments pinned on my front for all to bear witness to. I was returning to Papa and Solange accomplishing what I had intended; finding my own way and hopefully myself in the process. But I had no idea of the self that awaited me in Marseille.

Chapter 6 – Home and Then Home, Dec. 1919 – Apr. 1920

I arrived home just before the winter holidays. Papa and Solange welcomed me with great affection and quiet relief. It seemed I was never to be out of Solange's sight those first few weeks back inside our house. She fed me all my favorite foods, did my laundry, offered to prepare my baths and wash my hair. I, who had been caretaking for so long, did not know quite how to react to my sister's kindnesses. While I understood it was her way of reassuring herself that I was safe and sound and truly home, as well as wanting to make me feel welcomed and cared for, it was disconcerting at best.

I felt a great settling in at the core of my soul to be back in our home, my room, and with those I loved so dearly. I realized I also felt very much a visitor and while acknowledging that this was certainly a natural feeling after four years away, I wondered when I would again feel at home in this house.

Those first months of 1920 (actually through that winter into spring) I was content to remain with my family keeping much to myself. While Solange and I did go to town once or twice a week to the markets and prepared our meals together eating quietly with Papa when he was home, I was not eager for further social interaction. Time and again I turned down the many good-intentioned invitations either from friends from before my time away or friends of Solange's that now wanted me to join in their many activities. My declines were always accompanied by explanations regarding my continued fatigue and weariness; quiet and rest being what was needed for a while longer to restore me to myself. And this was certainly true and everyone "understood", but it was also more true that I desired only solitude and within that solitude I found a place of largesse that became my center and I did not venture beyond that place. Indeed I found myself retreating more deeply into a confusing despair as the weeks passed.

Apart from social invitations, no one asked me any questions. No one seemed curious as to what I had been doing as a nurse during those four years of war or what my experiences were and no one asked what my plans were now that I returned home. I later learned that Solange had told our friends and acquaintances not to make any inquiries of me. Talk was primarily focused on what husbands and young men had returned home, who was pregnant, and other post-war gossip that inspired women's talk. Most wives were once again out of the working environment and solely restored to their domestic duties. And, I assumed, were attempting to become pregnant and repopulate our country as was the official decree often heard from the government. Women could now return to "their rightful places". To my ears, conversations often sounded loud and boisterous with talk of the high prices of all goods, many of which were unavailable. During the infrequent times when I was with Solange and her acquaintances, the talk almost certainly came round to the topic of now that the war was over and women had served capably in so many capacities that there would surely be "greater equality for women". Many of my sister's friends held to the belief that men could no longer dispute the role their wives, sisters and mothers had played in France's victory. Women successfully replaced men in the factories and shops, served as nurses, were drivers in the military and on and on. Some of the women expressed the desire to continue working and some were unwilling to give up their jobs just because their husbands were home.

I pretended to listen, nodded when I thought it was appropriate, and offered no comments for, in truth, I had nothing to say that would relate to the present concerns of these women. Their eager post-war enthusiasm left me drained and seeking escape as soon as possible. After what I deemed as time enough spent in their company to be polite and with a look of understanding from Solange, I would either walk home alone, or if we were entertaining in our home, would retreat quietly upstairs.

My painting room, where I had spent so many wondrous hours, was just as I had left it. The windows let in all the sun possible in those days of late winter. Sitting in those familiar chairs under the windows, the sun warming all of me gave me reason to hope that the words I used to assure others that I was doing well would become my truth. That I would soon be filled with energy and some renewal of vigor. This room became my place of retreat, but the smells of the oils and turpentine were unfamiliar. The bright paintings stacked against the walls could not possibly have been created by me, and although I picked up the clean brushes and stroked the clean bristles, moved here and there the paint-stained spatulas, and pushed my fingers one by one into the dried paint on the palate, I could not imagine inspiration would ever cause me again to lift brush to canvas.

Many hours were spent there sitting in the long-familiar chair facing away from the window toward the center of the room. Sometimes I dozed off or would attempt to read, but the pages never held my attention. Solange would bring me tea, sometimes sitting with me for brief chats but mostly she left me alone. After those first few weeks home under her watchful eye and having restored some meat to my bones, she left me to myself to "sort things out". When Papa was home I made more of an effort to join the family. I convinced myself he had no worries regarding what he referred to as my "readjustment ". And when I excused myself early from after-dinner conversation with these two I loved best, he would rise from his chair, embrace me gently and comment that anyone could see I was still "ghastly tired". I knew that Solange by this time was beginning to suspect there was more to my retreating than just fatigue.

Solange and I each slept in our own rooms. Grown women would of course. During my first month home with nothing to fill my mind or tire my body, the little I did sleep was anything but restful. I began to have nightmares. Many nights I awoke in Solange's arms, shaking with fear and soaked in my own sweat and chilled to the bone. Each episode brought her running to my room; her quiet words assuring me that I was safe at home, and nothing could hurt me now. She would sometimes stay with me until it was first light or until I once again fell asleep. I would awake many hours later alone and wondering if the nightmares were real and had Solange actually come to care for me in the night. We never spoke of these frequent nighttime occurrences.

I began to dread going to sleep knowing what was on the other side of wakefulness. I suffered guilt as well, knowing that my nighttime terrors now involved my sister. She was becoming fatigued from worry and lack of sleep. As we prepared each night for bed, and as I had shared with her my fear of falling into sleep, she began to come into my room and rather than wait to comfort me in the midst of terrible dreams, we gradually began to talk about what we had both been experiencing these four years apart. We shared together night after night, week upon week, and what we told one another were not the inconsequential tepid comments shared in our letters back and forth during those years of separation. Those letters functioned as safe lifelines keeping us connected but not revealing anything that would cause one another worry or concern. Now we were truly safe, together once more, and could both let loose of four years of what had been left unspoken and talk of the ravages of war and the cost that had been paid.

Solange, knowing intuitively that what I had experienced, as evidenced by the night terrors, would be hard for me to disclose, began first to share. She slowly unraveled all that had occurred first in our city of Marseille during those years; the devastation of so many families as word came of the loss of a husband, a father, a brother, a son. Some nurses from town lost their lives as well. With so many of the men gone, businesses and shops had to be closed. There were extreme food and fuel shortages, and women with children that had no way to provide for themselves, were helped by those who could. My sister was at the heart of these efforts with Papa's full support allowing her to keep many widows and children warm and fed. She talked about the people we knew and cared about – who was lost, who came home, who came home but never completely returned, and on and on she shared.

As Solange patiently listened, I spoke about my work in the field hospital sites and the years nursing in Paris before I came home again. I talked as well about my nurse friends, the doctors and the patients I came to care about so deeply. Our stories caused us to both laugh and cry. Even greater was the sense of relief that came with honest reflection. Honesty with one another and more importantly with ourselves. I thought of my physician-counselor and his encouraging me to put into words the feelings and impressions from those experiences.

Little by little, those years were relived between us. Those nights of sharing and letting go became our own private world in which we found acceptance, release, and reconnection. We would begin talking as soon as dark fell and speak through most of the night, either in my bed or hers, and then sleep late into the next morning's hours.

She told me that shortly after I left for field nursing, Papa suffered what she called "an attack" and for months his memory seemed confused, his speech sometimes slurred, and his limbs weak. Our long-time physician assured her that with rest and good care, he would most likely recover his faculties, but he needed to begin to lessen his business obligations. During the many months of his recovery, Solange dealt as well with all the management of the business. Papa did recover but he forbid her to write me of this difficult period. I knew what she did not say — that worry for me most certainly contributed to his stress at that time and possibly to what I assumed was a small stroke. These weeks home I saw no evidence that Papa was anything but healthy — certainly grayer and a little more "stove up" in his joints, as he would comment, but still the same Papa as when I left home. Solange had retained her business responsibilities after Papa resumed work again knowing her continued involvement would lessen his stress and allow her to keep a close watch on him. She enjoyed the work and found she had a keen sense of business. She had truly become a business partner with Papa in every sense of the word.

During the war years Solange and Papa's lives were hectic with business, community concerns and constant worry regarding my safety. News coming from the north did nothing to dispel their fears. Papa was constantly seeking news from the northern front from any source he could. As the battle of Verdun began and raged through those long months and knowing I was somewhere in the middle of it all, both Papa and Solange were in constant terror that I would not survive.

Solange's admissions regarding their concern for me while at the front provided me a safe segue way into what became my revisiting of all that happened to me during that time at the front. I told her about the deaths of Dr. Bisset, Jeanne and Annette. About the smells, the sounds, the blood, the shells, the wounds, the surgeries, and the men I hoped we saved and those that we could not. I told her of my constant fear and worry and my anger. I was caught unaware as that anger rose up as bitter bile as I spoke to Solange of the devastation of war; the slaughter of the men, men on all sides of the conflict, and what I so strongly believed was the futility of it all. Solange would still my shaking hands when I became distressed and began to wipe them up and down, up and down my nightdress. After these weeks of nightly discussion, my nightmares became more infrequent and I began to sometimes sleep through the nights.

During February I wrote letters to Dr. Bisset's family and to the parents of Jeanne and Annette. These missives were long and much overdue, but it was only these many years later that it was possible for me to extend to them my condolences. I continued to miss them terribly and they were often in my dreams. They were gone and I was left, having no idea of what was to become of me.

The lightening of the malaise that I brought home with me began to allow room for contemplation and stirrings of my old restlessness began to seep into my consciousness. I did not feel ready to resume hospital work again and, truth be told, did not want to fall into the predictable life here in Marseille with the same predictable people. I did not have the energy to become what was expected of me.

As the winter of 1919 came to an end and spring was looked forward to, I saw in those around me an eagerness for the coming season for it was another sign of continued renewal. A spring in which the world was thought to be in a peaceful place. Seeds for the future could once again be sown and life could begin to move forward.

Surrounded by this semblance of hope that I did not share, I began to feel uncomfortably out of place. I continued my smiles and nods assuring everyone that, of course, I was feeling almost ready to resume "my old life" and would soon be inquiring into a nursing position at our hospital. They all smiled and nodded in return. Of course, Solange was never fooled and I was honest with her in every regard as to my current state of body and mind. She knew I was still fragile in many ways and was not in the least interested, nor did I have any intention of nursing at our local hospital. As well, I had no inclination to assist her and Papa with the business, nor did I care in the least about the social aspects of post-war society. So what was to become of me? Neither she nor I had the slightest idea. Papa, however, came unexpectedly to my reluctant rescue.

My gallant efforts at assuming a countenance of normalcy had not fooled Papa in the slightest. I should have known that he always had his finger on the pulse of our family and sometimes knew Solange and myself better than we did ourselves. And certainly Solange and I thought we knew Papa better than he knew himself!

In early March after dinner with the three of us, Papa brought to the table a small bottle of fine sherry he informed us he "had tucked away in his office for just such a discussion". Along with three small glasses that tinkled as he held them between the fingers of one hand, he poured us all a glass of the dark red liqueur.

My ears instantly picked up on his words and asked, "What do you mean 'such a discussion' Papa?"

He looked into his glass watching the rich liquid swirl round and round before lifting the glass, inhaling, and at last taking a long sip. "A discussion about what is next for us all My Dears. Now that the world has tilted on its axis but appears to have remained in orbit, we too must take a look at where we also have landed after all the chaos. I for one am ready for some changes and I want to hear from you both what you want to do, to be, and to become now that we are all here together with some time to spend in the contemplation of possibility." With that, Papa took another drink from his glass.

Solange and I were sitting next to one another across the table from Papa, and as we looked at each other and before either of us said a word, Papa spoke again, and again, his words continued to surprise us.

"I have a few thoughts. Ideas really and options more or less. I have worked for as long as I have memories. Life has been generous and rewarded our family with good health, a fine education for you both, good friends, a home and most importantly, one another. Nothing is more important to me than the both of you. For better or worse, these last years in business have resulted in affording us a future secured with monies invested and monies saved which will outlast us all. We can now think about what we could not have thought about during the chaos when the possibility of no future was a reality. But it is over. And now we need to make some practical plans." Papa smiled and conveyed to us with a gesture of his hand, an invitation to speak.

Solange took her first sip of sherry and then asked, "Papa, I am so relieved that this not a discussion regarding bad news such as financial ruin or reports of any ill health. You are fine as regards your health?"

"Yes, yes! And what is left of my life, our lives, I want to know we will spend it in relative safety, and fulfilling what have been plans and opportunities always promised somewhere in the future.

"And what do you mean by plans Papa?" I asked.

He turned his eyes to Solange. "Do you remember Solange, every time I left to go away, how you plagued me with urgent requests to take you along? You must remember asking me for as long as you have memories as well, for it has been all of your life."

"Yes, Papa", Solange said with a laugh, "and I still want to go along each time you leave."

"And that is where the opportunity lies My Dears! We must give ourselves permission to visit in our minds where it is and what it is we would most like to experience and then make it reality. I know my travels have taken me to those places you both studied diligently in your books. I could only send or bring you trinkets and items home that might lend you some sense of what these places were for me. But now we can go. Travel together to wherever it is we would like to spend time. Should either or both of you want to go with me, I would most certainly like to travel to America. Do you remember me speaking of my younger brother Antoine?" he asked.

"No Papa," Solange said as I met her look of consternation, "I don't believe you have ever mentioned you had a brother. Why have you not told us this before?"

"It is a long family story and one my family regarded as a blight on the family name. But Antoine and I are all that is left of my family and although he left France 25 years ago, we have remained in communication. He left a young wife shortly after they married, and subsequently was disowned by the family on both sides and fled for reasons I have never fully inquired into, he fled to New York City. He has had a prosperous business in commerce as well, and now that I am relinquishing my business here, I am most interested in investing in Antoine's burgeoning business in America. He wishes to expand and I only want to invest and reap the financial rewards. I do not intend to become in any way involved in the running of any more business."

Papa, always the pragmatist, took a deep breath and continued talking. "Placing our monies outside of Europe at this time and investing in the future growth in America seems wise. We will go to war again, this last conflict merely dampened the flame. I have every intention of making a safe haven apart from any future conflict that will most likely tear apart the fabric of our culture to an even greater extent than what we can possibly imagine. " And with that last statement he sat back in his chair, pursed his lips, raised his eyebrows and drained the last of his fine sherry.

Glancing at Solange, I could feel her body almost shiver in anticipation of a lifelong dream of travel becoming reality for her. And then her body stilled as she quickly glanced over at me. She well knew that traveling for travel's sake had never been an endeavor I aspired toward, and I would not find Papa's proposal appealing. But I remained still and quiet, thinking how I would possibly fit into these plans.

Papa, of course, saw this flash of understanding occur between Solange and myself. And, of course, he was prepared for this as well.

"And you my Marie. My brave warrior, my artist, my daughter with her mother's soul; I know these dreams of far travel have never been your own. But your future is yours to do with what you will. This is always our home and you can remain here in Marseille working as you might want….or not. But you have another option, a gift really that has been long in coming, awaiting for your arrival at a place where it would be received for what it was intended, a gift perhaps of refuge, peace and new beginnings." He smiled and reached over, placing his warm hands upon mine.

"What are you talking about Papa? What do you mean a gift?" I spoke quietly with caution and curiosity wanting him to quickly tell it all.

"Your mother, Marie. She left for you her family's summer home. It is north along the river Meuse some kilometers south of Verdun. I cannot know your feelings regarding anything that might lay in the north having been through so much there. What I do know is that the house is standing in one piece, is in rather good condition, and sits directly across from the river bank. There are no amenities; no running water or electricity but my man who took a look in the past month assures me the stoves on both floors are in good condition as is the one in the kitchen. The pump works well and the house stands much as it has for the last 50 years. This house in Meuse is where your Grand-Maman would take your Maman and her brother for most of the summer every year of their childhood. You own Maman, my own Edith, told me countless stories of the summers she spent there in what she referred to as "perfect bliss".

Papa paused now and with the soft voice of memory said, "After we married, your Grand-Maman gave the house to your Maman as a wedding present. She and I visited the house just once shortly after we were married and before you were born. Over these many years, from time to time, I would have the house looked at and each time it was reported to be in good condition. I did not know how it would be found after the war but to my amazement, I am told it is in excellent repair."

I sat there in our dining room just staring across the table at Papa and wondering what to make of what he just told me. His words I heard but could not begin to fathom what they meant or what it was he expected me to do with what he had just imparted.

"I have a house you say Papa? A house on the river Meuse?

"Yes Marie. And it is there waiting for you at any time in which you might decide to pay it a visit. I am not suggesting that you go there any time soon, but now seems the proper time to let you know of its existence. It may come to mean nothing to you, or you may become curious and want to see what your Maman bequeathed to you."

He stopped there and quietly looked in my eyes. "But Marie, if you do make the decision to go to Meuse, you will do so with your mother's name as your own. You will be Marie Durant only. Chagall will need to remain in your past as you look to the future. The future of anyone named Chagall with any link to Judaism, may come under suspicion. This war has stirred sentiments of long-seated animosities and fear. When conflict comes again, and it will, it will do so fueled by intense revenge and obsession. Germany will not long suffer defeat and when it moves again, we will have moved on."

Papa rose from his chair saying, "There is a great deal for us each to think about. Let us sleep soundly and talk again about this all in a few days when I return from what will be my last business venture. I have one more bottle of sherry to share with my girls as we make our plans." He came round the table, kissed us each soundly on both cheeks and retired up the stairs.

Solange looked at me and giggled. Actually giggled. A sound that was so infrequent and so joyful that I found myself laughing at her lightness. Obviously a great weight had been removed from her. We both erupted into overlapping sentences acknowledging how happy we were to know that Papa was at last ready to retire from his affairs. I knew she too would relish the release from the burden of business.

I spoke the next words hoping they would release her from any responsibility to me that might cause she and Papa to delay any plans for their adventures. "I may travel as well but only as far as Meuse to at least see where Maman spent so much of her life. I might find something of mine there, you never know. Did you know about the house Solange?" I quietly asked.

"No, Papa has never breathed a word of it to me. I do not think it was an easy gift for him to deliver knowing it might take you away from us again. But what Papa says is true, now is certainly the time for you to know and make your own decisions." She rose in mid-yawn, kissed me goodnight as well and went up to bed.

I remained at the table for quite some time trying to grab hold and make some sense of all the emotions vying for acknowledgement. My Maman. I felt she was reaching out to me. Still caring for me knowing that even now I would sense her watchfulness. The river Meuse. I did not know it. Had not seen it during any of the time I spent in the north. It would be new to me and yet knowing my mother had been so long in that place, might it also feel familiar? An unexpected gift from my own Maman. The reassuring words I just spoke to Solange for her benefit might be truer than I knew. As Papa said, we needed time to spend in the contemplation of possibility. I drained the last of the sherry from my glass as I toasted my Maman.

Chapter 7 – To Meuse, May 1920

During the time Papa was off on what he told us was his "last business venture", Solange and I spent almost all of our time discussing what Papa had shared. He left the day after our talk at the table, leaving so much unexplained, but with the express instruction that we continue thinking about "our options". Solange moved forward with complete confidence in their plans to travel making tentative arrangements for she and Papa to first venture to Spain and then to Portugal, leaving sometime in May. She queried me daily as to what I was thinking might be my own plans; would I be going with them, stay in Marseille or was traveling to Meuse even an option? I would respond daily that I was continuing to think about it all.

"There is no hurry Marie. No need to rush into anything you are not sure you want to do," she would say daily as well. But I knew there was a sense of urgency.

I did know that I would not be traveling with her and Papa. The most reasonable option would be to remain in the house in Marseille; at least for a short while as I continued to ponder the possibility of a visit to Meuse. It was extremely difficult even to think about the energy it would take to do anything at all other than to sit in my chair in my paint room. But I knew I must come to some consensus as I was sure Papa and Solange would not leave until they felt I was of a clear mind to either stay in Marseille or go north to Meuse. How in the world could Papa offer me such a "gift" that I was in no way ready to receive? Before he left the next morning, he whispered in my ear, "Have courage!" I was afraid I was going to let him down. I had had courage once, but thought I surely must have used up my allotment for life. How do you dredge up courage or even the semblance of courage when there is only a deep well of oblivion?

I took to taking long walks alone down along the harbor. The days were becoming warm and the constant breeze off the water was welcoming. I would stand at the edge of the water and close my eyes, imagining the great sea wind moving through my mind and my body clearing out remnants of remaining pain and repairing scars. Could a cleansing wind make enough room for the courage to do what I longed to do? To be brave once more and return to the north in anticipation that I might find there pieces of me that could make me whole? Truth was when I left Marseille I was a seventeen year old girl wishing for independence and adventure. And here I was again, thinking of leaving but this time in search of meaning and peace. In that span of six years so much had occurred, and I felt in many ways much older than my twenty three years. Could I dare hope that in those years away I developed reasoning mature enough to make a wise decision? But Papa wasn't asking me to be wise, he was asking me to be courageous. I thought there may be a great difference between the two.

By mid-April Papa and Solange were packing trunks and had their travel arrangements in place. They were leaving the last of April for Spain with no plans other than to travel to Portugal at some point and then on to America. Regardless of my decision to stay or go north, we would keep the house in Marseille. Papa had made arrangements with our solicitor and should I leave, the house would be looked after.

In the midst of their packing and arrangements, Papa informed us that he had asked this same solicitor to update his will stating the house, his holdings and investments were to be left equally between Solange and myself. Neither Solange nor I wanted to hear any of this for it was extremely unsettling. Why was Papa thinking it was necessary to have all this in place before they left? He also gave me a large envelope containing what he called "my new papers". I felt he was assuming that I had made the decision to venture to Meuse; that I had made the decision to become Marie Durant.

And thus, not knowing if it was Papa's silent prompting or my own true decision, I began packing my belongings as well. But where Solange had several trunks, I packed only one. I had learned that I needed very little in life and desired even less. I still had not spoken my intentions out loud, but by my very actions of sorting and packing, we all realized I had made the decision to travel north. Papa and Solange were bustling with eagerness to begin their adventures and I too allowed myself some feeling of anticipation. And so I called this feeling courage. I would make it suffice.

The day before Papa and Solange were to travel by train to Spain, they took me and my single trunk and one large tapestried bag to the train station and saw me off. Solange had placed bills of money Papa insisted I take with me in small muslin bags. She had sewn them closed and placed one by way of a belt round my waist beneath my dress and another on a heavy string round my neck. I was to wire Papa to send more money as needed. I did not count what monies went into those cloth bags, but knew it would be more than sufficient to get me to Verdun and then on to the house in Meuse.

Leaving them on the platform watching Solange's eyes stream with tears and Papa's face held tight against his own uncertainty, left me feeling totally bereft. They were sending me away. I reasoned I had no other option than to leave. I did not want to go with them, but I could not stay behind. And here I was steaming back to the source of my despair. Why did Papa not travel with me? Why did he not take me to where he wanted me to go? I felt unloved, completely alone and, at that moment, I could not have cared less what happened to me. I had been abandoned by the only people I loved.

I slept much of the journey north arriving at the station in Verdun in the early morning several days later. Papa had arranged for me to be picked up and delivered to the house in Meuse. To that end, I was met by an old man with an old truck. He told me Papa had sent a wire instructing him to take me to whatever establishments and shops were available where I could procure an assortment of whatever I deemed "necessary for a comfortable visit".

With palpable reluctance, the old man walked me from the station to the market as I assured him I needed little else than food. He said he knew the house, that it was empty and how was I to cook and what did I plan to sleep on? I acquiesced and between several shops, I purchased a single mattress, bedding, two kerosene lamps, oil, matches, a few pots, dishes and cutlery. Between looking at what I had assembled and his own judgment regarding what he considered necessities, he continued to add to the burgeoning pile of items stacked higher on the counters. I gave the goods little attention. While I paid what seemed an exorbitant amount, I did pause to wonder why this stranger would even care what I purchased or did not. Then I realized that not only had Papa sent him instructions to pick up and deliver me, he most likely had sent a list of what this stranger was to make sure I purchased to make my visit "comfortable".

Moving back and forth across the town from shop to shop, we loaded the items into his truck, one purchase after the other over a period of three hours. It was obvious by that time that the driver was as tired of this chore as I was, and I made the decision we had what was "deemed necessary" and what we didn't find, I wouldn't need. Tying it all down with rope laid back and forth across the overflowing bed of the stranger's ancient vehicle, we began the drive south. Papa had shown me on a map where the house was approximately located. Taking the map out of my bag, I showed my escort where I thought it was we were going.

"I told you I knew the house. Checked it out myself as your father instructed me to," he said sharply as he kept his eyes straight ahead on the road. He looked as weary and tired as his old truck sounded.

I sat back resigned to an unknown fate keeping my eyes steeled on the map in front of me and trying not to look around at the ruin across the landscape that gave evidence to the reality of my previous experience here. Recovery and rebuilding would take many years. In the town we left on our way south, people were bustling in what appeared to be endless energy continuing to reassemble their towns and homes and put their lives back together. Watching them filled me with a sad weariness. I was not sorry to drive away toward the country.

We drove for over an hour with me thinking every ten minutes or so the truck engine's horrible noises would result in being stranded with this cantankerous old man. Looking over at my driver, he took a dented silver container from his shirt pocket. He opened the tin of tobacco without taking his eyes from the road and wedged a large wad of the black strands up into his gums. What didn't make it to his mouth lay peppered across his shirt front. Yes, my Papa had abandoned me to strangers and a wasteland in every sense of the word.

The further we drove south and turning east toward the river, we began to see open fields of land that appeared to lay undisturbed from the last years of carnage. The Meuse ran wide and then would narrow with poplar trees scattered along its banks. As I began to settle into the winding of the river as we followed it south, my driver told me we were almost there. Ten minutes then passed when he pulled the truck to a stop beside stone steps that lead up a gentle incline to the porch of the house. I looked up at the house to my left and then to my right as the sound of the river competed for my attention. It was easier to keep my eyes on the river's flow than to turn back and take in this house.

"And here we are Mademoiselle. I have the key to give you. We'll unload your goods and I'll be on my way". It was dusk by the time we hauled everything inside depositing all the items on the floor of a large room just inside the door at the front of the house.

"My name is Bernard and should you need me, just ask anyone in town." He extended his fisted hand toward me and as I reached out to meet his hand, he dropped a large silver house key into my open palm. It was cold and heavy. He bid me adieu and left as if in a great hurry to get away. I heard his motor start with a loud bang and off he drove leaving me alone and exhausted.

The light was almost gone as I pushed my trunk to one corner of the front room, drug the mattress up against the wall under the front window and left everything else in heaping piles against the opposite walls to be dealt with tomorrow. Pulling a blanket from one of the piles, I laid down falling quickly into sleep. My last thought was one of relief - relief that I was alone and had no one I had to make an effort for. Not Papa, nor Solange, nor friends and certainly not for Bernard. It was enough of an effort to just be with myself and I would begin to deal with me tomorrow.

Chapter 8 – Cleaning the Rooms, August 1919

As I sat outside on the front steps with little around me but an old shawl, I thought again the chill was unexpected for such a late summer day. I realized my only comparison of what might be typical or not of August weather was the hot and windy August days of Marseille.

I knew the cold could come quickly here further north and that would soon require my thinking of a source for securing winter wood for the house stoves. As I gazed out beyond where I sat on my front steps and looked all around, I saw few trees of any kind, other than the river's poplars standing in such a straight line along the bank. Certainly there were trees somewhere nearby that would supply an ample supply of wood for the stoves. Bringing my thoughts back to today and the flowing fields of late blooms of lavender and the constant humming of the bees all around me, I vowed to enjoy the last of these summer days. When I arrived in May, the days were just beginning to warm and the relief in finding myself alone was so great and the returning despair so numbing, I was not aware of any sensations of cold or warmth, day or night. Sitting here in the bright light of late summer, I felt just the beginnings of my own thaw.

Disturbing these tranquil thoughts, I heard the pedlar Henri approach from the South before I caught sight of his donkey and wagon. He had been stopping every two weeks or so since I arrived. He had sold me six chickens shortly after my arrival and I had been exchanging their large brown eggs with him for bread and cheese. As was our usual conversation, we politely discussed the weather and what I needed to purchase and since I had no means of transportation to travel to town, he also brought my mail; the welcome messages from Solange and Papa. Accompanying stories of news of their travels, Solange sent money each month and often a box of trinkets or personal items such as handkerchiefs, teas or a small piece of jewelry such as a brooch. It reminded me of Papa sending us treasures from exotic places. Now Solange was doing the same. I took to displaying the items she sent arranging them by arrival on a folded blanket on the floor of my front room. These items were the sole sparks of color and whimsy within my world. I never wore the jewelry and used little of the money. The money I did spend went to purchase items from the pedlar; essentials I needed to sustain my life here. The larger amounts of money from Papa that Solange had sown into the small muslin bags remained in their cases and tucked into the back of a kitchen drawer.

With her letters, Solange always sent a blank piece of paper and an envelope addressed to where she and Papa were planning to remain for the next few weeks. I knew she was desperate for news of me; news that I was indeed in improving health and that I felt safe. She never inquired about my returning to the house in Marseille nor did she suggest I join her and Papa and for that I was grateful. I had written them each month in the four since my arrival in Meuse. With each letter I assured Solange I was intact, felt I had made a wise decision to visit this place, thanked them for the money or the box and to be sure to relay to Papa my love and gratitude. With each letter I sent back to them, I requested that a smaller portion of money be sent to me the next time or even no money at all until the first of the year as I had more than enough to keep me until then. My days moved quietly and with complete predictability, one into the other, and there was little to write that a reader might find of interest. Other than expressing my gratitude and my love – and the state of my chickens, there was little else to say. I realized it was solace for them just to know I felt secure in this place I chose to come stay. That, at least, I was always able to convey with no hesitation.

As the pedlar and his donkey approached, I stood and with a wave of my hand and a shake of my head indicated I needed nothing this day. I moved to turn back toward the house when the pedlar waved his hand above his head and called, "Wait Mademoiselle! I have news for you!"

I could not imagine what it was he had to tell me, but waited where I stood till he came along the front of my steps. Did he have a box or letter perhaps?

"Good day Mademoiselle! Are you enjoying this cool afternoon?"

I told him, yes, that it seemed early for such a fall-like day. It passed through my mind to ask him where I might secure wood but not today.

"Mademoiselle, thank you for receiving me this morning. Do you know of the convent just an hour so north of here?"

I told him, no, I did not.

"After the conflict these Sisters at the convent gave much needed care to men too sick to immediately return home to their families. They are a small Order and can only house and care for no more than five or six of our brave soldiers at a time. These men have wounds to the flesh and while these Sisters are many times able to tend to their physical maladies, many of the men have grave wounds to the spirit as well. While the Sisters can ease the pain of the flesh they cannot care for those men whose spirits are severely wounded. The Sisters believe that with time and tending these spirit-wounded men will heal sufficiently to travel home to their families. That is why I wanted to speak with you today Mademoiselle. You have empty rooms here, no? You could care for perhaps three of these brave men of ours, no?"

As he finished this long soliloquy, the most words I had heard from another person in my several months here, I just stood and looked at him thinking that surely I had not understood his question. He stood waiting, looking at me questioningly and I realized, that yes, what I heard was indeed what he was asking.

"No!" I told him. Although I had attempted to yell this word at him as emphatically as possible, it only reached him as a whisper caught in my throat. I could barely care for my own basic needs! I had nothing to offer these men. I told him again with more voice this time that I would not under any circumstances be able to accommodate these men.

"It is only three men Mademoiselle. Men very young and completely alone. The Sisters say these men do not talk, do not yet walk again and make no demands. They would only need to remain in their beds and you have bedrooms, no?"

I had not ventured often to the upstairs of the house. Had not even been curious to open the doors to what I supposed to be bedrooms. I had had no need to know what was above me as I existed only in the space below. Apart from the table and bench in the kitchen and my mattress and trunk, there was no other furniture in the downstairs and I had no recollection of any furniture in the landing above.

"No, no, no!" I emphatically told him again. This would not be possible. There was nothing I could do.

"Please Mademoiselle. The good Sisters need your help as do these young men. In return the Sisters say to tell you provisions would be supplied to assist in providing care. Provisions such as wood for the coming season as these men will need warmth. As will you Mademoiselle."

Did this man know of my coming winter's need? Was this a conjured scheme to secure my acquiescence to this unthinkable plan?

Again and again, I told him no. It was not possible.

"Mademoiselle, the good Sisters asked me to help secure a place for these three souls and I told them of your large home and that I would merely ask. I will let the Sisters know of your consideration."

Consideration? It was not consideration but adamant refusal! Thinking that the end of the matter and with a fearful suspicion I would not entertain, I quickly turned my back on Henri, this curious meddling persistent pedlar-man, and walked decidedly back into the house.

Shaking and barely able to reach the kitchen's darkness, I fell onto the seat of the wooden bench and laid my head on the table to subdue the rising nausea. I could not look into eyes of misery again. Could not give any touch of comfort for it would matter not the least and they would die regardless. No, I had nothing to give and the very thought of the attempt sent fear throughout my body. I swallowed down the rising bile in my throat struggling to shut away from memory the long-suppressed visions assaulting my senses.

Who were these young men once full of passion and eager to begin the battle? Battle for what? For what had they truly fought? I knew these men. Knew they believed zeal and a demand for justice would insure the righteous would be victorious. Knew we all believed these sacrificed millions who moved to defend and protect us from evil would surely be surrounded by cloaks of impenetrable righteousness and return home whole and healthy to heal our parched lands.

Was the victory worth the sacrifice of those scores upon scores of young men lost to battle? Lost forever was a generation upon whom we had laid our destiny; our men, our future, our leaders, our fathers, our brothers, our husbands. We were left with our land free of the evil but with losses so wretched we could not savor the victory.

Later that day I ascended the creaking stairs of my home; dust mites in rays of light leading the way upward. Around the broad landing were what I assumed to be three bedrooms. The doors were all closed and the rooms waiting. One large room in the northwest corner and two smaller on the other side of the landing stairs.

The top of the stairs opened into this broad L-shaped landing that was wider to my left; to the north. Straight before me at the top of the stairs was a large window framed in decorative lead with views long-looking to the west over the land; my land. Not for the first time, I was caught amazed that this lovely land was truly mine. Nineteen hectares Papa had told me. The view was captivating. Today I wanted to move through this window and fly across the blue waves of lavender before me.

How long I stood looking west from this window I do not know. I felt a settling down in spirit, gained a grounding, and turned to my left. I walked from the top of the stairs across the large wooden floors of landing which seemed a common area where people might have sat round the stove. This second floor wood stove stood settled onto a slate slab identical to the one on the first floor centered directly below this one. A large pipe of metal extended from the one below to this second one above and on up and out the ceiling. Both stoves were square, heavy cast iron and simple in design without ornament and with a locking handle on the glass-fronted doors. There were no ashes in this one as there were no ashes in the one below when I arrived. Whoever left the house however long ago left nothing behind. Not even the ashes to indicate life had ever been lived here.

The doors to the bedrooms were closed. I had not opened them on my one previous venture upstairs months earlier. Had my mother also walked the empty house closing these same doors before she left for that last time? I felt a strong sense of her; of a mother I never knew but knew had loved me. How long and with whom had she lived here? Without realizing I had moved to the closest bedroom, the one in the northwest corner, I found my hand on the doorknob turning it round and moved myself just inside the largest bedroom. Did I just imagine the air rushing round me escaping as an exhalation after having been so long cooped inside? Holding its breath until someone returned to breathe life into this empty house again?

There were windows, closed windows, directly across from the other on the east and west walls. A heavy wooden bed frame bare of mattress lay just to the north of the west-facing window. The bed frame had been pushed up tight against the wall, the foot of it ending just at the edge of the west window allowing whoever lay there some view out. Looking still from the doorway, a dresser of the same light-colored wood stood against the wall beside the bedframe. It was mid-height; three drawers high on two wide curved legs. The surface lay empty. To my immediate left stood a matching small round table and two chairs. These same light colored pieces of heavy wood matched even the planks of the flooring and seemed parts of the whole as though they had grown up from the roots of the floor. For whatever reason, the presence of furniture caught me by surprise. I had expected the rooms to be completely empty. I had not expected evidence of lives lived here. Evidence that my other family had been real. I felt a deep longing for these people of mine that I had never known.

The sun had decided at the moment to move from behind a cloud. The thin layer of dust which had been disturbed when I opened the door, floated in the air appearing alive and moving in the afternoon light pouring in from the west window. Looking round once more to make a whole of the pieces, I turned and left this room which I now thought of as "the first bedroom".

Now that one room was exposed, I could move to the other two perhaps better prepared to meet an unknown past. I proceeded across the landing and entered the bedroom in the southwest corner. Other than one bed frame of the same light-colored wood in a corner of the room and a west and south window, this room was otherwise empty. I came to call this room "the second bedroom". With the exception of dust made visible in the sunlight from the windows, the third bedroom in the southeast corner of the upper floor was entirely bare.

This was weary work – opening what had long been void and empty. My fear that I might find the rooms filled with personal items from my family was abating. Finding only the few wooden pieces of furniture and nothing more was welcomed with great relief. Emptiness was familiar and required nothing of me.

That evening I walked again up the stairs looking long out the landing window at the lavender flowing to the horizon just as the sun began its descent for the day. The lavender was in full vibrant bloom. In another few weeks it would begin its late-summer fade. My magic carpet I could jump into from this window.

Early the next morning found me watching the morning light through this same window, the blue-purple hues coming awake in the fields. With the sun came a breeze like life moving across this land; waves upon waves of a lavender sea. I could not deny the joy I felt each time I looked through these panes. My breath caught as the light found and held all of me through this window.

Feeling a sense of mounting obligation to do justice to this house, to offer what gratitude I could for this gift of mine, I began to clean. Not because I was entertaining any thought whatsoever of occupants, but rather because I wanted my entire house in respectable condition – top to bottom. Thus with mop, rags and a steaming bucket of suds in hand, I climbed the stairs and filled my soul with whatever it could store from the dawn's light and began to scrub each room in the order I had assigned them. The first bedroom, then the second and third. The landing was scoured last beginning with the stove now freed of webs and dust.

While I could not empty my soul of all that made it feel scarred, it felt good to me to remove from this upstairs all that had lain dormant in the dusty remains of a past. And the windows, all the windows up here, especially my large window in the landing, were free to once again admit the light and the shadows. The landing and bedrooms now damp and smelling of wet wood from the scrubbing, I made my way on hands and knees scouring one step down the stairs at a time. I stood at the bottom of the stairs on my first floor out of breathe, my long-dormant muscles letting me know they were ready for a rest. Afternoon had settled in, the time had passed unaware as I had entertained no other thoughts than ridding every upstairs space of dust and webs. As I stood there looking up at my work and feeling a sense of great accomplishment, my stomach began to rumble. I was hungry. Really hungry! Something I had not felt in such a very long time.

A week had now passed since I last saw Henri the pedlar and I was expecting his return any day. I was not looking forward to his additional pleas, his harping about my caring for the returned wounded. While yes, the bedrooms were clean, I had done so for me and not in any anticipation of them being filled with damaged souls. Besides, there were only two bed frames and no mattresses.

Henri arrived the next day asking how this day found me. I saw his eyes take in my rough red hands for I had continued my manic cleaning to include scrubbing thoroughly all the downstairs as I had not done before, especially the long unused-kitchen with its dust-layered shelves, drawers and wood cooking stove sprinkled with rodent droppings. That wood burning cooking stove alone took me hours. All the windows upstairs and down now gleamed and allowed in light through every pane. The lingering smell of the vinegar I used to make my windows shine remained in the house as well as on my hands. I loved coming in from the outside to be greeted by that pungent scent.

"You have been working hard, no, Mademoiselle?"

Did he miss nothing this prying man?

"Yes", I quickly told him and went on with a further harried explanation, "I have been cleaning. Cleaning my house because it was about time I completed the long over-due task. However, the rooms remain completely unsuitable for residents. There is a complete lack of furniture, two bed frames only and no mattresses at all, not to mention lack of linens, bedding, food stores and all that would be needed to provide adequate accommodations for nursing care."

I paused to take a breath I could not quite catch and hurried on, "It is not at all possible to tend ones so needy with nothing more than empty rooms! Surely the Sisters understand these men need to be sent somewhere more suitable. Caring for them here is not a responsibility I can even remotely consider. This is an outrageous idea and not to be entertained in any way!" Out of breath again, I felt my tightly fisted hands held taut to my sides looking, with as firm a face as I could muster, forcefully into Henri's eyes.

"But empty rooms are exactly what is needed! There are no obstacles here Mademoiselle! Your list of needed items are small considerations that can easily be accomplished." He said he was going north and felt certain he could locate what I indicated my rooms must have to make "adequate accommodations".

"I will return in a week's time Mademoiselle for the Sisters say to tell you the men will be arriving in less than ten days' time. We will need to work quickly but, with the cleaning done, all we need are another bed frame and mattresses."

Stomping my foot and filled with frustration, I shouted, "Henri, listen to me! That is not all that is needed! How can you possibly secure all that is needed; mattresses, linens, towels, soaps, bed pans, a hanging line, pots, pans, food and medical supplies?" And on and on the list flowed from my mouth.

"Yes, yes. These things will be found," he said calmly, the absurdity of the situation seemingly not penetrating his senses!

"Perhaps not all at once," he went on, "but we will find what you need to begin and you only need to begin Mademoiselle. The Sisters will provide at least one change of bed linens, clothes and other provisions, including a large supply of winter wood of course."

"Henri, have you even seen these men?" I demanded to know.

"No, no. What would it matter? What is most important is that you are well and ready to tend them and nothing more."

Mon dieu!! What was happening? Shaking and nauseous once more, I quickly passed Henri my overflowing basket of eggs and he in turn extended a basket with its contents wrapped in white linen. With a grunt of dismissal, I hastily grabbed the basket from his hands, almost dropping it as its heavy weight was unexpected. I could not meet his eyes, but turned and quickly retreated into my house. This time I did not seek the dark kitchen, but hurried up the stairs to my clean window in the landing. I folded to the floor my head pounding and held it my shaking hands. Slowly the fear and astonishment at what was about to begin faded as I realized I smelled a familiar fragrance causing my mouth to water. Was I always hungry these days?

Unfolding the white linen and looking into the basket Henri had handed me in return for my eggs, I found bread, cheese and two oranges. Large bright colored orbs whose fragrance had caused me to pause in my worry. I sat in an incandescent pool of bright light which had warmed the wood of the landing floor and using the linen from the basket as my spread cloth on the floor, I laid out the store of food. I pulled apart the bread, tore a chunk of cheese to place atop it, peeled an orange eating it quickly licking the sweet juice dripping from my fingers, and thinking there was nothing to even be concerned about. Henri would never find everything that was needed to allow me to care adequately for these soldiers and, truth be told, I thought him smart enough to know that this idea was both foolish and flawed. And all else he might be, I did not think him a fool.

Chapter 9 – The Men Arrive, September 1920

Henri did not return in seven days but nine. During that time, restlessness and anxiety found me endlessly pacing; outside, inside, upstairs and downstairs – again and again. No daily walks to the river as I might miss hearing his approach.

That ninth day he came mid-morning traveling from the north. As I looked down the road, he had what appeared to be pieces of wood strapped to the top of his wagon and across the back of his donkey were long stuffed packs wobbling left and right with the donkey's swaying steps. My heart fell realizing that all he hauled was to be delivered at my doorstep. Where would he have ever have found what was needed? From whom did he get these supplies and who paid the cost? These questions would come to my mind time and again over the next many months, but they never found way to my lips and Henri never volunteered answers.

As he rode closer, I was ready with harsh words. But as he got nearer, his wasn't the face of someone jubilantly succeeding in a mission, but the face of someone who was dreading rejection mixed with deep lines of fatigue. He stopped the wagon and as he sat and I stood, we took measure of one another. I can only imagine what my countenance reflected. Surely he saw my face change from determined steadfastness to one of confused empathy. As he jumped down from the wagon's seat to the ground with a heavy grunt, he turned and faced me. He was slightly taller than myself, but we were close enough in height that we were near equal.

He was expecting my refusal, but hoping for acknowledgement that what he brought in offering would be accepted. I realized that I too was waiting for my own acknowledgement. I realized I had days ago acquiesced to this scheme, but he could not know that. With only a nod of my head indicating hesitant willingness, I said, "Let's see what you have brought."

He began to unload pieces of a wooden bed frame, but before he could lay the first piece to the ground, I lifted one end and together we carried it to the house and up the stairs. The beams of wood felt too light to support a body, but perhaps together the whole would be more substantial than each piece. The wood was dark and old. It was highly polished and obviously had been a fine piece at one time. I wondered and quickly decided that most likely, Henri had cleaned and polished it hoping I might find it suitable. Once we had all the pieces upstairs and into the second bedroom, we fit it together easily. I wanted two of the men to share this second bedroom room keeping the third for storage and what supplies I would need close at hand rather than running up and down the stairs. Even as we carried the furniture into place, I was continuing to acknowledge that, indeed, I had given this much thought and had the space carefully planned out and allotted. Now with two bed frames in the room we moved the heads of the beds against the west wall with enough room between for a table that Henri carted up from the wagon.

We then unloaded unwieldy stacks of linen from inside the wagon, each of us carrying a heavy pile up the stairs setting it on the floor beneath the window. I went for a second. Henri did the same with the landing now strewn in unmatched worn fabrics of differing weights in shades all browns and beiges. The blandness had an unintended calming effect on me and aroused no turmoil as the piles of cloth were harmlessly unintimidating. I could not differentiate the intended use one piece from the other for it merely appeared as one large massive undifferentiated pile. Henri assured me there were two changes of linens for each bed, clothes, towels, washcloths, blankets and other assorted items that might be needed. We then went back down and struggled for the next hour to haul three ungainly mattresses in various states of repair up the stairs and onto the bedframes.

With nothing further to haul up the stairs, Henri took the liberty to look about the landing, moving to each of the bedrooms standing as I had done at first, just in the doorways. His eyes travelled over the clean emptiness of each room.

"Windows in each room. Morning and afternoon sun. Good for healing and this long landing will be a place for them to exercise; to stretch and walk about. Of course not at first, but in good time, no?"

All I thought as we headed back down those stairs was this was as bad an idea as ever conjured by good people.

Once outside, we stood by the wagon each contemplating the days ahead. I told Henri I needed food staples and had the money to pay (thank you Papa). That day, and insisting that he take my money, I purchased from him dry beans and flour, salt and sugar, soap and saucisson. Henri said I also needed yeast as he assumed I would be baking bread, and handed me a lump of wet fragrant yeast wrapped in a damp cloth. He also pulled from the depths of the wagon a large wooden box containing, he said, salt pork, dried fish, potatoes and onions. Without waiting for any comment from me, he picked up the box and carried it to my front stoop. I stood holding the yeast taking in its fragrance that caused memories to waft through my mind. It was all I allowed my mind to think about.

Solange and I had often spent much time in our sunny kitchen watching and chatting with Cook as she made bread. We even tried, when Papa was away and the help released for a week or two by Solange, "at full pay of course" she would always tell them, to follow Cook's recipe and make our own bread which was never quite up to Cook's.

Henri had lifted several more items from the wagon and these were lying about me on the ground. He and his donkey had brought so much! And now he would be leaving again. Leaving me with all this and my not knowing where to begin to sort it all out.

"Three days from now. I will return in three days with your men." He said as he climbed aboard his wagon.

My men? Three days?

"And with more provisions of course Mademoiselle Marie. Sisters will send along what they also deem necessary for the care. No worries Mademoiselle Marie for you will do them justice."

Henri's donkey turned at that moment of my doubt, looked into my eyes and with a shake of his head, let out a low bellow. He seemed to be telling me it was alright. Desperately needing something to hold onto, I walked over to this weathered dusty grey and brown animal and flinging my arms round his neck, I buried my head in his sun-warmed hide.

Three days. Three days. Who was I to dispense justice to anyone? These men were damaged. There would be no justice for them now or ever. And most certainly there was none in my power to bestow. With those thoughts, I reluctantly let go of Donkey and bid Henri adieu.

In three days a wagon came from the north. Not Henri's boxy closed wagon, but one open and flat. Wide enough for three men to lie side by side I thought. Henri sat atop this first wagon pulled by a large brown horse. I assumed the horse and wagon must belong to the Sisters at the Convent. Donkey followed along behind pulling his usual load of his own wagon. Donkey's back was again piled high with items strapped, tied and hanging all across his back and sides.

They came slowly. Were the men injured still even of body and not just of mind and required that no jarring or running over ruts should occur? I waited on my steps next to the road, my hands shading my eyes for a better view of what was to befall me.

"We need to get them inside. They are hot and moaning." Henri said as he swiftly jumped from the wagon seat and hurried toward the back of the wagon and the waiting men.

I eased myself forward to look into the wagon. The men were there beside one another laid head to foot and foot to head. Young, very young; two all strawberry blonde and freckled. Another darker of hair. All of medium height and all looking severely emaciated. All had their eyes closed and were still of body. Only a low moaning emanated from them. From one or two or three of them? I could not tell but this moaning was a sound familiar to me. I heard it my sleep. Saw in my sleep mounds of men laying in each other's blood and crooning a plea for death. So much of the time there was nothing, nothing, which could be done. My own moaning often merged with theirs and some mornings I still woke myself up with the sound. Would these men now wake me up as well? All of us awaking together in a chorus of torment? As Henri began lifting the first of the men out of the wagon, the one of darker hair, I moved without hesitation to assist. Again, what else was there to do now?

Henri said Sisters thought this man was named Laurent. He could walk just a little if assisted. With support from Henri on his left and myself on his right, we managed to half drag the weak man into the house and up the stairs to his assigned room. I gave him the first bedroom – the northwest room. Maybe he would soon be able to sit at the table to take his food. And then soon thereafter be able to leave.

After settling this first man onto the bed, we proceeded quickly back to the other waiting men. Together Henri and I lifted one man at a time their slack bodies from the hard bottom of the wagon. As I gripped their thin-as-spindles ankles and with Henri's hands beneath their underarms, we moved as quickly as possible to the house. With great care, we slowly climbed the stairs and placed each man atop his own mattress in the second bedroom.

They were, the three of them, dressed in heavy wool pants and thin long-sleeved shirts. All torn, stained and missing buttons.

Battlefield leftovers clean but scarred. An outer covering for what lay identical beneath.

I asked Henri if they had each a change of clothing.

"There is one jacket and another pair or two of wool pants. Sisters had nothing else to spare. It is fortunate they are all of one size, no? And there are gowns among the linens I think."

I had made up the beds days ago and sorted through the linens placing them in separate piles of blankets, sheets, towels and clothes on the floor of the third bedroom. There had been only three bed gowns, two pairs of pants and one shirt among all the linen. I emphatically told Henri that only loose fitting clothes were to be secured and thick linen pads for the beds had to be found. No wool garments. Only cotton linen that could be washed and dried quickly.

Seeing my look of frustration, he immediately assured me this would all be found. The Sisters told him none of the men were able to use a chamber pot on his own and Sisters said the men often soiled themselves. Henri must have known something of what this caring entailed.

"I understand the urgency Mademoiselle Marie! Truly I do." I believed him and believed he was certainly glad to be the one securing the garments only and not changing the beds.

"And a drying line Henri. Did you bring a drying line?" I asked as we stood peering into the third bedroom at the meager sorted piles of bedding, towels and clothes sitting along the floor against one wall.

"Oui! And I have more soap Mademoiselle Marie. The drying line can be hung out back by the pump. I will see to it before I leave.

And also I brought a large wash tub and wash board. Your pump is situated well for the laundry, no!" My only hope for sustaining changes of clean dry laundered items for each man was the hope of warm dry days.

Checking on each man once again, we found them quiet and I covered them each with a thin blanket. For all appearances, they were sleeping peacefully. We moved quietly down the stairs and out to Henri's own wagon. He had untied Donkey who was now standing in front of the flat open wagon as if ready to have his goods unloaded off his back.

And unload goods Henri did! Henri unloaded baskets strapped to Donkey's sides and wooden crates of dried foods, fresh foods, breads, cheeses, oats, more flour and vegetables. Even dried apples and honey from the convent Henri said. Oh my! My kitchen shelves would be full for the first time.

Henri placed it all on the ground and looking at this bounty, I wondered if these men high above me would even be able to eat. Surely any means of sustenance would need to be soft and moist and little at a time. I understood that Henri did not just bring these items for the men. They were again offerings of atonement to me in exchange for what he and others perceived to be my good heart and capable skills in caring for these men.

Henri last brought forth another basket. It was white wicker in a rectangular shape with handles woven into the sides. He lifted it gently by those handles and laid it on the drop-down back of his wagon. The basket was filled and overflowing with clean white towels.

"Mademoiselle Marie, I did not forget you said some time ago you needed towels for yourself. Here are towels for your use alone and also a small token of gratitude."

He began to slowly pull the towels apart seeming to prolong his own excitement with the hope that I might feel a sense of anticipation as well. Among the towels was tea set of thin bone china! Henri carefully laid each piece out on the wagon lid; four delicate cups placed atop four matching saucers. The blue flowered pattern was very reminiscent of the tea service Solange and I used all my years of growing up in Marseille. I was quite moved by this gift and more by this man's thoughtfulness on my behalf.

Clearing his throat, Henri said, "The kind woman who so generously provided this china set said she did so for the benefit of aiding in any way the recovery of your men. She could not however spare her sugar tongs but, as we have no sugar cubes, I told her all the better, no?"

Smiling at Henri's remarks, I wondered if the thick white towels were coerced from this woman's own home as well. Four of them, as though they were additional pieces of the tea set. And there was also a tin of loose tea leaves. "China tea", Henri said as though an afterthought.

He quickly rewrapped the delicate china back into the soft white layers of the towels placing it all gently into the basket. Presenting the basket to me with a slight bow and a soft "adieu", he made as if to leave.

Sudden fear of abandonment suddenly assaulted me. "Henri, wait!" I said stepping forward as if to stop his leaving, "I need to know when you will return. What if I need something urgently for one of the men?"

"I'll return in three days of course. This time with wood!" he said with a smile and then did take up Donkey's reins and departed.

Surveying the items laid round my feet, I began carrying into my house what I knew were donations and contributions that Henri secured from what I hoped were willing people. I saw that among the array of goods there was a chamber pot. Now I had two. This chamber pot Henri brought today was cracked but large and low and would be put to good use. This pot would belong to the men, and I would keep mine as my own. At times I had the feeling Henri most likely bewitched others to do his bidding – much as he bewitched me! Hopefully he had not snatched this pot from beneath someone unawares.

I carried the food stuffs into the kitchen laying it all atop the wooden table then arranging the items across my clean empty kitchen shelves. All other various and assorted items sat on the floor in the sitting room. Where to put it all? I had no shelves other than the ones in the kitchen and those were now full. No armoires for storage either. It would just sit where it lay and I would sort it all later moving everything to do with the men to the third bedroom above.

It was now early evening and checking on the men once again I found them still sleeping. Coming upon each one silently I was once again struck by their youth. Laurent, occupying the first bedroom, looked the eldest of the three. Looking again at the two other men, boys really, I thought once more of how alike they were with few differing features one from the other. Could they be brothers by blood as well as battle?

These men were known to me. They were my kin, my fellows from the trenches. I felt safe in their shared despair. Despair so entrenched in the soul it would be easy, so preferable, to die. I had been there with them. Knew the sights and smells and sounds they could not face. This sleep kept their minds locked safely away from the conscious reality of despair that awaited them. I felt a sudden rekindling of compassion at the sight of these skeletal boys. But no, it was not compassion. It was selfishness; a fake empathy. I had no other choice but to say yes to Henri and the Sisters' request to care for these Boys. I was to be a parasite feeding on their anguish to keep me alive. Perhaps by saving them I could save myself as well.

Chapter 10 – Laurent, September 1920 – June 1921

Through fall and into November Henri passed often on the road to and from Verdun. Sometimes stopping and sometimes passing through. Being busy with the men, I did not always see him as he traveled past my house. Evidence of his fleeting presence was found at least twice monthly and, as often as every ten days, in the provisions he left just outside on my front door stoop. Foods, and sometimes clothes and linens for the Boys, were often among the items he left for me to find. I always had ready a basket of eggs for him to take and left these outside the door around the time I thought he might pass. Mingled among the more general supplies he left, I would also find a treat or an item I knew he felt might be appreciated or helpful. Two red apples, a square of dark chocolate or perhaps a fragrant tea. Once a new knife, sharp and long, and once a new razor to shave the Boys. I always imagined these as bribes. Small treats to keep me from throwing up my hands and his finding the Boys outside my door to cart away rather than my basket of brown eggs. But every surprise was appreciated and often caused me to smile and, yes, there was anticipation.

Henri's passings often felt clandestine. Did he not announce himself thinking perhaps it would interrupt my care of the Boys and my constant washing, cooking, feeding, changing and cleaning? Yes, it would have interrupted my day, and how welcomed it would have been! Someone to talk with, and not just to talk at, would have been appreciated. I sometimes felt as though Henri snuck off quietly to preclude any chance of my reneging on this commitment to tend. Once again, I felt abandoned.

It's possible Henri passed unannounced believing my daily routines and constant patterns of tending were rituals aiding my own healing, and therefore not to be disturbed. Not even for welcomed company. I would most likely, in those early weeks with the Boys, have complained bitterly; haranguing Henri with protests and angst. It wasn't fair that all this care fell to me! And with no help from him! In my own fear and feelings of helplessness, I would not have recognized his continual gifts and provisions were evidence of his continual watchfulness and affirmations regarding my own abilities. As my days were physically exhausting, there was little to no time for thoughts of self and less for self-pity. I sunk into dreamless sleep each night never waking myself again with noises from the past.

Most days were organized around feeding times. I truly thought of them as feeding times and not meal times. Mealtimes were to me events shared round a table with others who actively participated in the passing of foods and the sharing of conversation. Mealtimes conjured memories of dinners with Solange, Papa and our frequent guests, their smiles of anticipation reflected brightly in the candles gracing the long formal table.

Feeding times with the Boys reminded me of feeding animals; initially, reluctant animals. I would make the porridge adding salt and sugar accompanied by cups of strong tea, carting it upstairs on trays and filling the Boys' mouths with spoonfuls of the warm mush. Some mornings I awoke more cheerful than others. On those mornings, when I could, I would greet the Boys with a hearty "Bonjour!"

The Boys in the second bedroom, so similar in all ways, I thought of as the Brothers and they were always attended to first. I would lay their food tray on the table and shake them gently, or sometimes not so gently, into a state of wakefulness. A least enough awake to slip the spoon into their almost always drowsy mouths. I would sometimes chatter about the food, the weather, asking did they sleep well, telling them the plan for the day and all of this in the time it took for me to feed one and then the other as their bowls emptied and they swallowed their tea. This morning feeding with these two Boys occupied 15 minutes of time. Initially they all needed their well-cooked sodden oats offered from my spoon and slipped into their mouths. This breakfast of oatmeal never varied and they seldom now refused to eat. Then laying the bowls and cups aside, I would wash their faces and change their pants leaving further ministrations until later in the morning.

Mornings and evenings were the busiest. During the first few weeks with me, they slept for most of every afternoon. Every other day I gave them full bed baths and changed their bed linens. On Mondays they were shaved - "Monday shaves" as I told them. I moved from one boy's tending to the next throughout each day, and each day moved seamlessly into weeks.

Laurent I would feed and wash after the Brothers. He appeared some years older than the other Boys and, unlike the other Boys, always seemed somewhat present. I sensed he could understand my words and had his own thoughts, yet he never spoke to me with anything other than his eyes. I would catch him surreptitiously watching me as I laid his own tray upon the table in his room or as I straightened his bed. I was never overly cheerful or chatty with him as I was with the other Boys. We seemed, both of us, to require and appreciate an honesty about the situation. Laurent tolerated my assistance and I sensed that he perhaps remembered something of what had occurred to bring him to this place. He often seemed so aware of his surroundings and yet restless and despondent. Could he see pain reflected in my eyes as I could in his own?

Laurent, after the first week of his arrival, began to flinch with each approach of my spoon, putting up his hand as though to deflect any more intrusion to his person. If he could lift his hand toward his mouth, could he not lift his own spoon? And he did. With hand over hand coaxing, he was soon feeding himself with no help from me other than constant encouragement to "eat it all".

As the weeks moved forward, Laurent's eyes remained pools of sorrow. Occasionally I saw a reflection of defiance at my constant and sometimes forceful promptings to eat, walk, wash and dress himself. He would succumb, I think, only to stop my unceasing nagging to walk further, eat more, put on his shirt, use the pot by himself and on and on.

To my mind, his efforts toward self-care demonstrated he was healing and perhaps soon he would begin to talk and tell me the name of his family. I encouraged him to try, telling him if he could, he would be reunited with them. His growing ability to meet his own needs allowed me more time to tend to the other young men who were little changed from when they arrived. While the Brothers spent their waking time with opened eyes, I do not believe they truly saw anything of their present surroundings or situation. The Brothers continued to cry out in the night during their sleep from dreams that were surely haunting. I continued to speak with them during their feedings and ministrations. While they would reflexively open their mouths as the spoon touched their lips, they never looked into my eyes or acknowledged my presence. Occasionally a spoon or bowl would slip from my hands to the wooden floor and they would startle or cry out. They never showed the slightest response to my words, their eyes remaining empty and their faces flaccid.

But Laurent I knew understood my words. He would sometimes, after I stated an opinion as to how he "wasn't really trying" or made a casual comment such as "wasn't it nice to see the sun today", bestow me a glance of either disdain, frustration - even mocking humor, but never did I see in those gold-brown eyes a hint of hope. And never a grunt, a groan or a harrumph much less a word did I ever hear from him. But he and I did communicate and often shared the afternoon tea together. He sometimes listened with patient eyes as I would describe the state of the other Boys or what I had just found on the front steps from Henri. I imagined that I was company for him and that he realized how very important it was that he recover and go home to a life I felt must be full of promise. There were people waiting for his return, and I would help him return to them. I was a nurse and he the embodiment of all I could hope to heal. His life would be salvaged from the waste and destruction. There would be hope.

In late October I caught sight of Henri from an upstairs window just as he stepped upon the wagon to depart. I flew down the stairs and out the door to catch him asking if he could possibly bring me chairs next time – three or four chairs. I wanted to set them on the landing at the top of the stairs where the Boys might sit by the stove for meals followed by exercise. Laurent was now able to walk alone. Slowly and with care, he walked himself around and around the landing twice a day as I worked with the Brothers. They were all gaining weight and growing stronger and with great physical support I was able to walk the other two about their rooms and knew I could walk them to the landing into a chair. There, together, might they show some sign of past acquaintance? Would some slight recollection be stirred if they were in close proximity one to another? Or just by one another's presence might they not be inspired to try harder? Henri said he would bring me chairs in two weeks.

Laurent would now independently use his chamber pot. I would find evidence each day that his food was passing. The other Boys, while often still soiling themselves, were beginning to acquiesce to the routine of finding the pot placed beneath them three times each day – an hour after each meal – one then the other. The constant surveillance of their hygiene, keeping them clean and dry, was my most challenging task. Although the Brothers seemed not to have any awareness that they were soiling themselves, I felt a loss of dignity for them that did not lessen with time. Looking in their eyes and faces, I hoped to see a sense of shame or apology; an acknowledgment that might move them toward self-awareness, that might hasten their movement toward skills needed to go home and be themselves. But as pleased as I was that Laurent was using the chamber pot, and the others most of the time with assistance, there was little to encourage me that any of the three of them either cared, or would eventually care, about what happened to them. I realized much of what I stubbornly regarded as signs of healing were in reality due to abiding by my strict routines. Still, I held fast to the any slight indication they were benefitting from my tending.

Henri brought my four chairs in two weeks' time. Four unmatched seats in many stains of brown; sturdy high- backed chairs with no side arms. We carried them up the stairs and placed them against the wall in the long L of the landing opposite the stove — two on the north wall and two on the west under the landing's window. I moved the small circular table out of the Brothers' room placing it between these chairs. For morning breakfast, the Boys sat in these chairs pulled close to the table. If I placed the bowl in front of Laurent and handed him his spoon, he would feed himself while I fed the Brothers. After these meals, Laurent would walk the landing passing beside me back and forth as I walked one boy and then the other. I took to singing songs, reciting poems and rhymes. Hearing the sound of my own voice was tiring and I would have thought they would be tired of it as well for no voice other than my own ever filled that landing.

At the beginning of November, after all these weeks of constant caring, habits were being formed as a result of my efficient daily schedules and routines. I truly felt progress was being made! They had gained weight, seldom soiled themselves and were able to walk with support. Laurent was even more independent. I now set a goal for them and for myself. They would be well enough to return to their homes for the winter's holidays. This I realized was as much out of my own selfish need to return to my solitary life as it was from a compassionate heart. I was becoming weary of being the only one holding out hope and often my constant care was frayed with impatience.

As the end of November approached, we took all our meals together on the landing followed by as vigorous exercise as I could extract from each of them. But if only they would give me some sign that they knew they were getting better! Show some spark of cognition; some desire to move out of their present state of apathy. But I continued to assume some sense of hope for us all.

My conviction that they all were headed home was rooted in Laurent's growing independence. Lately he ended his round of walking about the landing by standing at the top of the stairs looking down. Was he wanting to go explore the house? Maybe a walk outside? Although I encouraged him to venture downstairs with me, he physically resisted and would become tense at my hand on his elbow in invitation to descend the stairs. Shrugging off my hand, he always turned away back toward his room. Of course he was hesitant and most likely even afraid. For what would he find once he left this familiar upstairs abode? I could not know if he realized, as I did, that he would very soon be ready to move on.

I was doing my upmost to give them all I could; all I had. And while their physical needs were being met, I had little to give in the way of any emotional support. So on and on my words of encouragement beat against their ears. Why were they not trying harder? Did they not know I was sacrificing myself for them? I was doing them all the justice I could!

Each morning I felt myself reset. Today, I vowed, I would be more patient; not so demanding. Each morning as we began our breakfast routine in the landing, I recited to them the day of the week, the month and the year. What season it was and described the weather outside. I explained the plan for the day. Although "the plan" never varied to any great degree, other than perhaps what we would eat for dinner or that it was a Monday and that meant a shave. I hoped the constant grounding to present might begin to nudge against their pervasive emptiness.

Had their ability to be present left along with their spirit, leaving these bodies suspended here in a time and space they were not meant to be? If I dwelt on this, often what seemed the greatest reality during this time, I would wonder if I was not their protagonist prolonging their stay in this present hell. But on and on we went, for whatever else were we to do?

As December loomed close, and the days were short on light and long on length, I began to take the Boys afternoon tea once again in their rooms. I sat with each boy separately talking with just them for just a time. The days were cold and though their doors were left open and the stove's swirling heat flowed to each of their rooms, I knew they were warmest tucked in bed until our communal dinnertime and exercise in the landing.

Laurent always had his tea last as I wanted to believe he looked forward to this time; found the time socially pleasant rather than just a routine to be adhered to. I had begun to share with him stories of my life before the war. I still believed I saw a glimmer of cognizance, of some emotion, when I talked about my family in Marseille.

He would now on occasion look at me directly. Sometimes for long periods of time, especially if my own eyes were averted from his as I poured our tea or straightened his bedding. I know I asked too often for him to try and talk; to please attempt to tell me the name of his family. Could he but write it on the paper I provided? But he would stare at me and would neither nod nor shake his head at questions I asked.

By the end of the day, my own self tired and worn out, I felt Laurent was being stubborn and was purposefully annoying me. There seemed understanding beyond his eyes, but how was I to know? So on that day as other days, I took the afternoon tea tray to his room. As I walked in announcing today was chamomile accompanied by bread and jam, he was not in his bed. He was not in the room. I laid the tea tray on the dresser and moved back to look in the landing, calling his name. Although he still would sometimes stand atop the landing, I had never seen him attempt any movement to go down those stairs. Having just come from the kitchen, I knew he was not on the lower floor.

Moving back into his room, the faded yellow curtains I had found in the bottom dresser and had so recently hung with small nails above the window's frame, were rising and fluttering in the cold breeze flowing from the open window. How had I not seen that open window when I first walked in nor felt the freezing air?

How had I missed the rope tied round the foot of that heavy wooden bed? The rope extended out the open window with what I knew to be Laurent at the other end? I had not missed these signs when I first entered. My mind rather refused to acknowledge the unthinkable vision it conjured.

Standing as frozen in my place as was the air in the room, I could not look away from the flapping yellow curtains nor the rope tight and taut against the window's ledge. No movement could I make to that window. I did not need to confirm by sight what I knew lay against the house. I turned and closed the door hoping against hope Henri, now two weeks since a visit, would come quickly.

The other men did not receive their afternoon tea that day, nor the next. I was barely able to feed them their meals and keep them clean. All the daylight hours not spent in tending were spent pacing in and out of the house looking north and then south. Henri needed to come and come quickly.

It was two days now that Laurent was left dangling high in the frozen air. Henri came late the afternoon on the third day. While still a far ways off to the north, I waved with frantic arms and called his name to hurry, hurry. As he came close to the house, I ran to the wagon telling him what he would find behind the house.

Leading Donkey and wagon across the side yard round to the back and cutting through the dead lavender stalks, he maneuvered the wagon close against the house. Standing atop the wagon, he cut the taut rope and set Laurent free. Henri gently laid him out across the wagon's top and covered his body with a cloth pulled from the back and, with a length of rope, tied it all down.

I was dry of eye. Beyond this grief. Henri spent some time assuring me all would be taken care of. He wanted me to know there was no fault here, but the result of a decision made by Laurent alone. Henri said he would return in three days. I made him promise. Promise that it would be three days and no more.

"Yes, yes! Three days for then it will be December." I did not understand his meaning but only that he would soon return.

This is not how I wanted these Boys to leave. This was not justice! Laurent did not do justice to my ministrations; my tending. Self-righteous indignation filled me with anger covering the grief and despair I desperately needed contained.

I began over the next days to understand that Laurent had been biding his time. Waiting till he was physically able to climb down those stairs to secure the hanging rope. He would have seen me out his east window as late as the end of September into October hanging our laundry from that rope. Then too cold for hanging clothes outside, he could have seen me late in October taking down that rope and coiling it round and round itself, laying it on the stone slab next to the pump. In all the times since, when filling or emptying pots, pitchers or buckets, moving indoors and out, I had not missed that rope.

After two days I ventured into Laurent's room. I untied the rope wound round the bed's leg and burned it outside with the yellow curtains. Then I cleaned that vacant room. Scrubbed on hands and knees every surface, every corner till my knuckles bled and my bare knees were raw and splintered. The wood was wet and the mattress lay propped against the open window for airing. The bedding was washed and now lay hung all across the banister drying by the stove in the landing. This would become my room now and the morning of the third day the bed was freshly made and I vowed that I would sleep here every night. I was puzzled by my decision to take the room for myself. I only knew I must and by doing so was somehow a gesture of acknowledgement on both our parts. I trusted Laurent would have wanted me to have this room for my own. A room where we once took our tea together. I room that would not be left vacant even with his passing.

Henri returned as promised on the afternoon of that same third day.

"The Sisters arranged all for our friend Laurent. As they prepared his body, they much remarked on his improved state. For even in his demise there was evidence of your good tending Mademoiselle Marie".

I told Henri I was now going to claim that bedroom as my own. Henri nodded but said nothing. I could not meet his gaze knowing that there I might find solace, but could not risk losing my composure. Henri was leaving again and there would be no one to grieve with other than myself.

He asked after the other two Boys. We had not truly talked since the Boys arrived in September, but we now exchanged more words than at any time since. I shared with him that their physical state seemed well repaired but there remained still no sign of true life; no movement of the face or eyes to validate any presence of spirit. He said he would share all this with the Sisters as there were renewed efforts to reunite soldiers with their families. We talked specifically of their height, unique coloring of hair and almost golden eyes and how they so closely resembled one another. All this he would pass on to the Sisters in hopes of helping find their families.

He slowly unloaded more wood by my back door, wanting I think, for us to find that place returned to normalcy. After providing me with additional provisions, he climbed aboard his wagon with a quiet "Adieu". I gave Donkey a quick fierce hug as he began to pull weight of the wagon forward.

I sorely wanted to run after Henri asking when I could expect him next, but did not want to burden him nor acknowledge to myself my need and thus stood my place. I knew he would not be long away, but long enough for me to perhaps gain an equilibrium.

Turning my efforts to the remaining Boys, I exercised them now three and four times a day, sang louder, and spoke with more feeling. I no longer felt resentment or forced obligation for their care, but truly an emerging sense of empathy. Laurent's death had somehow moved me past a point in my own suffering. I could grasp hold of theirs, acknowledging them as separate sentient beings that somehow could be touched by compassion rather than betrayed by resentment and guilt. Laurent had taught me that I wanted to live. I did not fully know that until his leaving and this was his gift to me for the care I gave.

By March the Brothers were getting out of bed independently, walking the landing and pausing at the window to view the spring arriving. They were eating all their meals without aid, dressing with minimal help, and using the chamber pot when reminded. But still they had no voice but they had one another, and seemed content and even peaceful in one another's company. They no longer cried out in their sleep.

In early April Henri told me the Sisters thought they had made contact with the families of my two Boys. Based on the descriptions I provided, the families and the Sisters felt they found a match. They were indeed Brothers, twins in fact.

Two weeks later the Brothers rode away sitting beside Henri atop his wagon. Their faces were still passive but physically they looked well fed and healthy. Their families were travelling to the Convent where they would be reunited. I declined Henri and the Sisters' invitation to come as well to meet the families and, as I knew, to accept the gratitude they were sure to offer. I had no need to extend the goodbyes, but stood in the road and waved them on their way until I could no longer see the wagon.

What I was left with by their leaving was redemption. Redemption for both Laurent and myself. He healed to where he alone could make a choice whether to live or end his life. I tended him without realizing he moved toward a destiny he felt was his. Tended him until he was physically able to decide his own fate and strong enough to carry out his decision. And this was justice after all.

I wept then for Laurent and for all our lost men and their waiting women and families forever changed. I wept knowing that I had made a choice to live. Thanking those Boys for allowing me to find my own renewal as I tended them. Thanking Henri who seemed to know all things.

With the warmer days my spirit continued to thaw. It was a slow thaw, but I felt it at the edges. In early June I received a letter from Solange telling me she was coming for a visit.

Chapter 11 – When Solange Came to Visit, July 1921

The days before Solange's visit slipped past in silence and were undistinguishable one from the other. Where once the sound of my voice was heard continually speaking words of encouragement and songs had been sung with gusto to the Boys, now there was stillness. I felt as empty as the house. I kept thinking I needed to get everything ready for Solange's visit, but in truth there was really nothing to prepare. I had again swept and scrubbed the house, and the beds in the second bedroom where she would sleep were made up with clean linens. Other than the bedroom furniture upstairs, the house was still essentially bare of furnishings of any kind. At least the upstairs reflected some semblance of life being lived. Even if it was just to sleep!

Since the Boys left, the kitchen lay virtually empty and unused. I had little food stored and nothing prepared for my sister's arrival. Henri had been by a week before and I had not purchased much in the way of supplies or foodstuffs at that time. I did tell him Solange was coming and I would be needing to buy from him the next week. I had not seen him since. Solange and I would decide what we would eat when she got here. However, unless Henri came soon the reality was there was virtually nothing to feed my guest! I did not spend much effort in rousing myself to usefulness and, other than thorough cleaning of the house, had spent each day since receiving her letter, listlessly awaiting her arrival.

The joy that accompanied the reunion of the Boys with their families and my hope that the worst of my despair left with them was short lived. The long days of light and warmth surely should have spurred me to.... to what? Plant a garden (Henri offered seeds), sew curtains for the newly cleaned and empty rooms upstairs, take a book and my lunch and sit by the river?

The familiar malaise had gradually ascended over me. I did not know what to do with myself now that the house was empty again. Even knowing Solange most likely expected to see me well and productive hadn't spurred me to any action. "Productive" was a word she used a great deal when describing the attributes of one living a life in a "healthy productive manner". She knew I was expecting her, knew that I had once again had a house void of life. I had written to her and Papa more frequently during the months the Boys shared my house and she knew all three were now somewhere else but here.

Maybe I was just lazy and not truly fatigued. After the Boys left I had bumped the mattress from my room on the second floor back down to the first. The distance up and down the stairs mornings and night required more from my person than I had to give and it was much more difficult sleeping where Laurent had slept than I had imagined. Truth be told, it was difficult to sleep up or down. I just couldn't seem to settle my mind enough to drift off. Maybe it was too quiet. The last nine months of purposefulness and the constant company of others, even of those that were essentially silent, was extinguished with the Boys' leavings. Where once the solitude was healing, now it became oppressive. My old sense of restlessness could be felt gnawing at my edges again. I thought this perhaps a good sign as I would rather feel restless than useless!

I sat on my steps each evening looking over at the Meuse and waiting for Solange. The river's flow over rocks and roots was the sound that accompanied the beating of my heart and if I listened with eyes closed, I could hear the drying stalks of my lavender waving over and over itself in the gentle breeze moving across the vast fields. Solange's letter of three weeks ago said to expect her today or tomorrow – or maybe the next day. I found I was both dreading and eagerly anticipating her arrival. I wanted her to love my home, to love my land, my river, and to love me as she always had.

The next day arrived hot and bright. Mid-afternoon found me sitting once again on the front steps hoping for a river breeze when I heard the sound of metal on wood. I saw the dust rising before I saw the flat bed wagon. She was sitting high up atop the wagon's seat behind a muscular black-brown beast of a horse. She slapped the reins up and down as though she could see the prize in sight and drove hard to claim it.

Her dark navy wide-brimmed bonnet was tied with matching sateen sashes blowing wildly about her face. Solange driving a wagon and heading for my home! I could not help but smile! Ah, my Dear Sister, almost here to rescue me. I was thankful for the fourteen months of separation, for any sooner visit I could not have welcomed. I stood and waved wildly at her approach, filled with relief and an overwhelming sense that now I could rest and lay down in the presence of her good senses.

She slowed when she caught sight of me, reining in the horse as the dust settled down about her. Her slow approach allowed us to rein in our emotions as well I think; to look a little at one another from afar off and to perhaps gauge how best to begin our reunion.

She pulled the wagon close alongside the front where I stood and jumping from the wagon, out of breath as though she had run with the horse, she exclaimed. "I made good time. Actually having never driven a wagon before, I think it went rather well".

Folding me into her arms, I was speechless - not from emotion but from a wave of overwhelming weariness that settled over me. The dust stirred up by the wagon wheels was now clouding all about us filling our eyes and noses with dust. That is how I felt inside – dusty and dry and Solange was here to help clean out my cobwebs.

Moving only a few steps back from the wagon, we just sat down together on the steps gazing over at the river. We locked our arms and sat as close together as possible. The close warmth of her felt like peace before sleep came and I laid my head on her narrow shoulder. I may have dozed off for as the breeze came up, I quickly startled. Solange let out a small chuckle and patting my hands, said it was time to go inside. I knew there was no more delaying her look about my house and so we rose and walked up the steps toward the front door.

She walked expectantly ahead of me, moving with determined purpose and opened the door. She paused just inside looking left and right, up and down, and began slowly moving through each empty room downstairs. I watched as her eyes took stock of the barren rooms and all that was needed. There were tears at the edge of her words as she began making a verbal list of all we would need to purchase to fill these rooms.

Solange continued talking, making one-sided conversation, not disguising well her concern in finding the house looking so barren. I did not take on her concern as I was too caught up in the joy at just hearing her long-missed voice. I was taking pleasure in every syllable she uttered. It didn't matter that I neither desired nor needed more than what I already had. I realized that seeing the house through her eyes and knowing her opinion of what "every adequate home must have", my house appeared barely sufficient to sustain life. She hadn't yet realized there was no life to sustain. Or maybe the house told her its secrets and they were so hard for her to hear. But I let her go on and on.

"Papa was so wise to have purchased the wagon and horse and have it waiting when I arrived. He said it was about time you had your own means of transportation rather than having to constantly be relying on the Pedlar."

So the wagon with horse was Papa's idea – of course it was! I had no idea what I would do with my "transportation" but I did relish that the idea had been Papa's. Another gift that he thought I needed that he could provide. I had been very disappointed when Solange wrote that he would not be accompanying her on this visit.

She spoke of so many things we needed to accomplish that I finally ask her how long she was planning to stay and where was Papa.

"You know I left Papa in Portugal. We only just completed all the finalities regarding leasing the house in Marseille. We'll be sailing for New York in one month's time. We have no return plans Marie. I could not leave without seeing you, especially since it may be a long while before we return. I hope it is alright if I stay two weeks."

"Two weeks! Is that all after so much time apart? It will take you at least that long to tell me everything you and Papa have been up to and all your plans! Just two weeks before you leave and go to America?" I said with a lightness I did not feel. Hugging her again and looking into her eyes I said, "You know I may not let you go Solange. It is very hard to imagine that you will no longer be just a train's distance away from me."

"After two weeks Marie, I promise you will be sick and tired of my harping and nagging! But, yes, I am sad as well but am so glad we do have this time together. We will make the very most of it!"

She finished her walk about the front rooms and was headed toward the kitchen. I dreaded her visit to my kitchen. After the Boys' departure, my kitchen became barren once more in every sense of the word. I had once again closed the window shutters and it took on its former gloom. My kitchen never saw the light, never changed, was always reliable – never causing a shift of light away from a predictable center.

And here Solange went, "tsk-tsking", throwing open the window shutters and opening wide the back door. She surveyed the pump, the lean-to and shed where my nine hens were all stirred up by our racket and clucking louder than Solange was "tsking". How I had missed that sound! All my life, there was no end to all of the reasons she had to "tsk" at me. A sound of love.

She walked further out to the back stoop around the lean-to to where the fields began and with her hands on her hips let out a sound of "Ahhh" as she surveyed the lovely fields of lavender. She reached for my hand and we stood together looking as far as our eyes could see. I was so glad she too appreciated the loveliness of the lavender. After many minutes, she turned us round and we re-entered the kitchen, light now illuminating the wooden emptiness of that sparse room with its splintered old table and bench and spider-filled webs along all the empty shelves. Seeing it through her eyes, it really was depressing and completely drab without any color whatsoever. But I was protective of this room - this unkitchen - and I wanted it to continue to lie undisturbed for it was not yet ready to receive what it could not sustain.

"After we thoroughly clean and stock these shelves, your kitchen will be better in no time", she said as though she came to nurse my home back to health.

Before we went upstairs, I prompted her to bring in her belongings from the wagon. Later, I told her, we would move the wagon to the back of the house off the road, settle the horse in the lean-to and then take a walk along the river. She agreed and we went out again in the bright sunshine and began to unload a half-filled wagon of unknown items! First we unloaded her luggage and bags, including a large leather travel valise which I realized was a very old one Papa had used on his travels for as long as I could remember. I wondered if I opened it and put my nose inside would it smell of Papa? Would he then be here for just a little while?

Solange had also managed to bring two large rattan baskets of breads, cheeses, teas, dried meats and fruit. I assumed she procured these in Verdun after exiting the train and securing the wagon and horse. Together we also lifted from the back of the wagon a large wooden box. We had laid everything on the floor just inside the door. Now Solange pulled a large cloth from Papa's valise which we spread across the kitchen table and upon which she laid her baskets of food. That was a worry I could let go of for she had brought our supper…and breakfast and most likely enough food for many meals.

Standing in the kitchen looking back into the front room, her pieces of luggage, the wooden box and Papa's valise were strewn all about the front room. Seeing that room filled with so many items after so long being barren, felt to me cluttered and almost made me uneasy.

"And now to move the wagon and then to your river," she said, and we strolled leisurely out the door to the road keeping a good hold of each other. Now that she was here, my dependable take-charge sister, all seemed more right with the world. And now it was my turn to show her my world.

Together we led the horse round to the back of the house, unhitched him from his trappings, gave him a quick brushing and settled him into the lean-to with grain and hay, both of which Solange had in the back of the wagon. Two large metal buckets of grain and two bales of hay.

She climbed into the wagon and handed down the heavy buckets after which I climbed into the wagon with her and together we managed to heave the hay over the side of the wagon dragging the bales into the shed. I must admit it felt good to be doing work this hard and it was also surreal that I would be in the countryside in Meuse unhitching a horse from a wagon (both now mine!) heaving hay and lifting buckets with Solange. Without a word spoken, I knew when she looked at me, these same incredulous thoughts were going through her head as well. Who would ever have thought our lives would have changed so drastically from the ones we led together in Marseille? Another hug and brushing the hay from our clothes, we bid Horse and the chickens' adieu and set off for my river.

I was glad the afternoon was bright and shining, the sun's rays dancing around the surface of the river giving a festive welcome to my sister. I had brought my blanket from the house and we spread it on the grassy bank leaning our backs up against the poplar trees. The water gurgled over the rocks and for a little space of time we just sat listening to the river and to our own and one another's unspoken thoughts.

"Are you happy here Marie?" she asked.

I thought sometime before answering, "I am certainly not unhappy," I said looking out at the river. "I think I am mostly content. But since the Boys have left I must admit I am, while not really lonely, maybe wondering what I will do with myself. I feel somewhat at loose ends."

"Mmm. That makes sense you know. From your letters I wondered how you managed to do all of the care you did for them. And their laundry and cooking and everything else required besides the actual nursing. It would only be natural, after having been so occupied physically and mentally, for you to think about how you might now fill your days. It must be an adjustment."

"They left in May and here it is July and I cannot seem to find the energy to even think about what to do next. Mostly I just want to sleep. Is that strange?" I asked Solange.

"No, not strange at all Marie. You most likely need a good rest. And then of course Laurent; hopefully you know that it was not your fault that he chose to end his life as he did." She said as she placed her hand upon mine.

Letting out a long sigh and taking a moment to examine my feelings, I said "I have seen so much death and suffering and despite all the best efforts of myself and others, we could do nothing to save so many of them. I realized shortly after arriving at the front that I was not responsible for whether the soldiers ultimately lived or died. Nurses training instilled that reality in us all. We had to live that perspective otherwise we would not have been able to do our jobs. And I did my job as best I could every day. There is no question in my mind that I was a good nurse. My struggles now continue to be coming to terms with the extent of the dying, trying to answer questions about the necessity of it, and attempting to make some sense of it all. I am better able now, with the passing of time, to separate my nursing experiences from my personal emotions. But that presents other problems I can't seem to sort out. I keep asking myself if the war really made a difference. What did all those lost lives accomplish? It would be far easier if I could just fit it all together into a single compartment in my mind that said "professional nurse". I can't seem to do that and when I am not busy, as I am not now, my mind asks those questions again and again. I think that is what makes me weary. I am tired of the questions."

"Papa says all thoughtful people are asking those same questions Marie. Now that life has resumed some perceived sense of normalcy, Papa hears those conversations in the cafés and in the appointments he attends. It is interesting to spend time outside of France listening to people in countries other than our own not so affected by the conflict, reflect on what all occurred. Sometimes what I hear is offensive and I feel the fierce loyalty I have always felt for France. Other times I can't help but ask those same questions myself. As Papa does as well. The difference is you saw it firsthand Marie; your hands were bloodied by the reality of what was lost. And what was gained? That remains to be seen. I tell myself we are free from the tyranny that would have been had we not found victory. That is my only answer to the question of 'why'. Real or not, it is what I hold on to." Solange leaned back once more against the tree and closed her eyes.

Because of my isolation I had supposed it was easy to think that others may not have been in much the same state as myself. Once back in Marseille people had seemed jubilant at the war's end and rightfully so. I just didn't suppose they were as questioning as myself.

And then coming here there was no one to even discuss with the state of the world. I had thought I did not even want to talk about any of it but found that this conversation with Solange was indeed welcome. She gave me permission not to feel responsible for being the sole individual trying to make sense of a changed world.

Henri had offered to bring me newspapers, assuming I might want to know about what was happening beyond this home in Meuse. Also probably thinking a broader perspective outside myself might help alleviate my gloom. Maybe I was now more interested and ready than I had thought to resume discourse outside of my depressing one-sided internal conversations. Solange had only been here a few hours but already her presence and our conversation lifted months of dullness from my brain and body. The sun was settling into the river now and I was getting hungry. I kept imagining what lay in the baskets of food she left setting on my old kitchen table.

"Solange, are you awake?" I knew she wasn't, as I had earlier heard her breathing settle into the familiar sound of her sleeping. More than an hour had passed, she dozing and I lost in my own thoughts and just enjoying her here with me by the river. But my stomach had another agenda.

"Solange, wake up and let's go eat! I know you must be as hungry as I am!" I said shaking her gently.

"Yes, yes Marie!" She said with some annoyance at being shaken awake. "Is it always so peaceful here? What a wonderful place for an afternoon siesta. We must do this every day I am here."

Quickly agreeing, I held out my hand to help her rise. We shook out the blanket and headed toward the house. Again, I felt pride that my sister was enjoying already the solitude of this place.

"It is certainly a good thing that you brought food Solange as I had nothing to eat! I did expect Henri to be by here sooner so I would at least have something for you to eat!" I said as I began rummaging through the overflowing baskets.

"Oh yes. Henri. I want to hear more about this pedlar Henri and so does Papa. Why have you not purchased a cart or wagon before so you could go into town getting what you need rather than relying on a stranger? And, obviously you could do with some more household effects." She said looking around again at the empty rooms.

"Well, Henri stopped early on when I first arrived and has been doing so every week or so for all this time. I have never needed or wanted to go into town and have been perfectly happy securing what I needed from him. Really Solange, he has been a God-send. Especially when the Boys were here and I needed supplies and foodstuffs weekly for sure. He also brought me chicks so I always had fresh eggs to eat and for barter. There was little I needed apart from essentials and more often than not Henri supplied additionally what he thought I needed. And I can admit to you but never would to him, that he has been a constant source of goodwill and kindness. Of course I pay him, but he has never taken advantage and never asks me questions." I state all of this in what I think is a very matter-of-fact manner.

"I had often wondered Solange, if Papa had not somehow contacted Henri, paying him a stipend to keep an eye on me. Do you know if this is true?" I ask her.

"Ha! I wondered that myself when your letters describing Henri first arrived, but when I asked Papa he assured me he knew nothing of the man and has been quite concerned given Henri seems to be rather over-solicitous on your account. Truth be told, Papa is very much hoping I will have a chance to meet this individual and report back my impressions." she said with a half-smile on her lips.

I found myself laughing at the thought that Henri could ever be perceived as a suspicious character and told Solange so.

"He is well known to the Sisters at the convent an hour from here, as well as all those living north and south on this road. He has been, I think, in the business of "traveling commerce" as he calls it, for most of his life. But I ask him as few questions as he asks me, so I do not really know. I told him you were coming for a visit and that we would be needing supplies, so I really do expect him any day."

As if on cue, Henri and Donkey were heard on the road next morning as we were finishing our breakfast and making a list of all Solange thought we would need for the house as we planned a shopping trip into town via my new transportation. Anticipating Henri's momentary arrival, I experienced a twinge of nervousness in my stomach wondering what he and Solange would make of one another. Wondering also why it seemed to matter. I did know that up until this time, Henri made my life here possible and should Papa receive an unfavorable report from Solange, there might be difficulties.

Yes, I definitely needed this meeting of these two important people in my life to go well.

"Bonjour Henri", I called out loudly to ensure he would indeed stop and engage us. He smiled as I approached Donkey with my usual welcoming hugs and introduced them both to Solange.

"Bonjour Mesdemoiselles." Henri said removing his hat from his head and bowing slightly to my sister. I thought his hair was shorter, was trimmed and freshly washed perhaps?

Solange acknowledged his greeting and then we all stood as though not quite knowing what to say next. I felt anxious realizing that Henri and Solange were appraising one another without appearing to do so. My two benefactors face to face and me just standing there.

I had nine eggs held ready in my basket for Henri. Solange had helped me gather them that morning. I wanted her to see that I was indeed using some of my own resources to fend for myself.

"Merci Mademoiselle." Said Henri taking my basket and moving round to the back of the wagon unlocking the hinges to lay open the back. Henri often brought items unexpected and much welcome, and I just knew that because Solange had come to visit he might have more than the usual flour and cheese. And of course I was not disappointed.

"In celebration of your visit Mademoiselle, and your sister having told me you have not been to this part of France before, I have taken it upon myself to bring some items that are distinctive to this region of Meuse." He pulled from the recesses of the wagon a large box lined with a blue cotton cloth, the ends folded over so we could not yet see what lay beneath.

"The good Sisters from the convent close by send you jars of their honey with the express request that you take some to your Papa for his enjoyment as well," he said laying five small jars of honey on the wagon's lid. And then saying, as though it was a surprise to him, "Oh, I see the Sisters have also included three boxes of their beeswax candles. Twelve beeswax *bougies* in all. Not knowing if you had holders for them, I have brought you six *bougeoirs* as well. These seats for your candles are unmatched, but may you find them decorative as well as useful." He said this matter-of-factly but I saw the twinge of a smile playing round his mouth. I had told him many times that I did not need candles or candle holders as it seemed an extravagance seeing that I was seldom up after dark.

"How long might you be visiting Mademoiselle?" Henri asked placing the jars of honey and the candles back into the box and lifting it across the space into Solange's arms.

"Two weeks Monsieur." Solange said trying to peer into the back of the wagon.

"I hope then it will be my pleasure to see you again to bid you a good journey home before you leave." Turning to me Henri ask, "Mademoiselle Durant, what can I bring that you might need as I will be by again in three days' time?"

"Solange rode here in a wagon and horse that Papa had arranged before her arrival. Papa's gift to me! We are planning a drive into town as soon as we decide what we are needing. Solange is encouraging me to fill my house with household items she insists might make me more comfortable." I said with a smile and lacing my arm through Solange's.

"A wagon and horse is certainly a necessity for you if you are to continue living here Mademoiselle! You will find your way around town in no time and people will be most happy to make your acquaintance, guiding you as best they can to whatever you might deem necessary. Whether the items might be available for purchase is another matter. Much is still in short supply. Your Papa is indeed a wise man to have secured your transportation and your sister kind to make such a necessary delivery!"

Turning to Solange, he removed his hat once again, bowed slightly saying, "Bravo to you both and if there is any way in which I might be of assistance, I would count it my privilege."

He closed the back of the wagon, handed me another basket with what I assumed were the *bougeoirs* wrapped in heavy paper, gave Donkey a kind slap on his middle and jumped atop the wagon with a final, "Adieu, see you in three days' time," and was off down the road.

Taking our new items into the house and laying them on the table we had moved downstairs from my room, Solange could not resist opening a jar of the honey. Reaching into the basket that held the *bougeoirs*, my hand found a round loaf of crusty bread Henri had tucked inside as well. Running to the kitchen, I secured two plates, two knives, and as quickly as I cut thick slices of the bread, Solange lathered them with the sweet fragrant honey. "Papa will love this! And to think it is made here in the convent by the Sisters that live so close to you." she said with her mouth stuffed full.

By these words I knew she had given her blessing and acknowledged that a good impression had been made and all was right with my world. Solicitations from the Sisters via Henri and their gifts of the honey and candles, were evidence to Solange that there were others I had acquaintance with besides Henri. I knew that made her feel more comfortable that I was not truly alone here. I did not tell Solange that I had never visited the convent and had never met the good Sisters. I was thinking Henri was a clever fellow and, whether knowingly or unknowingly, had once more come to my aid.

We did not go into town that day, but went to the river after we gorged on our bread and honey, taking a long nap in the sun and finally finishing our list for what would be our excursion the next day.

As dusk approached and I prepared a light supper, I had Solange unwrap the six *bougeoirs* from the basket, discovering as I knew she would, that each was a lovely treasure. As I brought in our plates of food, she finished setting each candle into its holder, lit each wick, arranging the lovely pieces across the table. I would be sure that several of the *bougeoirs* made their way into her luggage. I was basking in more than the candle light reflecting on the many gifts bestowed on us that day.

Up early the next morning, Solange imparted to me that she clearly recalled how to harness Horse and attach him to the wagon and would instruct me on the finer points of driving. Truly the novice leading the novice! Thank heavens Horse was a patient and gentle teacher for he seemed to be guiding us to what we needed to do and how to do it! We three became fast attached that day as we rode that bumpy road north. Once arriving, we rummaged and sorted through shop after shop realizing anew that there was often little to purchase that Solange felt I needed that was within the budget I allocated for my purchases. I insisted on paying for it all, albeit from the monies Papa had given me when I first left Marseille, and would accept nothing in the way of payment from Solange. If I could not pay for it, it was not purchased. In this way I also made sure the number of purchases of furniture and other items was kept to a minimum as I truly did not want a house filled with items that meant nothing to me and for which I had no need. I also wanted only items that had been used. I had no use for anything that was new.

We finally found a moderately sized mahogany table for the dining area, four matching chairs and an almost matching cabinet. All the pieces were scratched and scarred and had obviously been well used. I immediately wanted them to find a new home with me. With a thorough cleaning and a heavy coat of beeswax polish, they would be restored and ready to be loved once again. Found in another shop, in the recesses of a back room which Solange charmed her way into, we secured a small divan, two padded chairs, two lamps and small round table of a wood the seller said was cherry. These pieces, though not new, were not so well used and Solange was triumphant at this find of what she declared was "very suitable indeed". My empty downstairs space, where all these pieces would live, would now be full. Too full for my taste, but I knew their presence would provide Solange with a sense that a life was indeed being lived in my house. If that eased her leaving and provided a good report to Papa, I was content. She had also insisted I needed warm clothes, and bought for me a long heavy coat and thick wool hat she said was a belated birthday gift that I would most surely need for winter when driving the wagon to and from town. I then purchased a slightly used pair of heavy boots, thick socks and a wool scarf. Lastly, we secured more grain, hay and a dark red heavy wool blanket for Horse, and eagerly headed home.

During the remainder of Solange's visit, we many times arranged and rearranged the pieces of furniture. She insisted we take our tea in the "parlor" as she called the east side of my downstairs area, as she wanted to remember us sitting there together. The west side of the room she called my "salle a manger" and where we placed the mahogany table and chairs. The pieces did look lovely under the window. The cabinet was placed against the wall that separated this larger open space from the kitchen. On a last foray into town, Solange found a set of "gently used" china plates with matching serving pieces, and many cooking utensils, including a flour sieve and rolling pin, she insisted I needed. I did like the china as it had a delicate pattern of flowers and nearly matched the cups Henri had brought when the Boys were with me. I gently placed each plate and cup into my cabinet and stood back admiring them through their leaded glass-front doors.

We had purchased enough food and dry goods that we did not again go into town, but spent our remaining time together in lazy conversation. The days were warm and most afternoons found us once again by the river enjoying the lovely solitude of this beautiful place that seemed more home to me than ever before. Shortly before Solange departed, Henri called upon us once again. That is the only way I can describe his "passing through" as he was very polite, solicitous, and after some time in conversation, bid my sister Solange a kind adieu. I knew that his timing was intentional and was grateful for his kindness toward my sister.

"Not a bad fellow this Henri," was all she had to say as we stood together, as I most often did when Henri left, watching he and Donkey as they traveled down the road.

I drove the wagon myself that last day to see her boarded on the early afternoon train headed west and back to Papa. Our visit had been more than I could have hoped. Our goodbyes were tearful, each of us reassuring the other that we would of course write as always, and with the promise that we would see each other in the not so distant future. Pulling away from the station and back toward home, I felt a sense of melancholy and some astonishment that she and Papa were truly leaving for America within the next few weeks. So far away from what they had always known. But had I not done the same? Moved body and soul to this new place far away from all that was familiar? And I had told Solange the truth, I was truly content. And knowing Solange had come and left and left bestowing her blessing on what I had chosen here, I allowed myself to fully embrace this place I had chosen as home. I did not know how my days would be filled, but I did know I had a horse, nine chickens, a wagon, a well-supplied kitchen and a home full of furniture to care for. That was more than enough for now.

Chapter 12 – The Sewing Box, October 1921

When Solange visited in July, she had brought with her the large sewing box from home. She told me she had restocked the box with new needles, many spools of thread, newly sharpened shears, my worn and perfectly fitted thimbles and "bits and pieces" she thought I would find use for.

Neither during her visit nor since her leaving, had this box been touched or moved much less opened since I took it from her hands and brought it into my house. Lifting it now, I again remembered it was very heavy; much heavier than I recalled from home.

The sewing box had beckoned to me these three months since Solange had left. It was a distraction that drew my eyes each time I passed it, lying so innocently atop my mahogany table. I began imagining its contents, thinking it would be stuffed full of lovely and alluring items of color and texture. But I was busy, much too busy to go through this sewing box and idle my time away with needlework! I had become quite good at making excuses for not delving into and exploring the contents of this sewing box.

Needlework was always a past-time we enjoyed. Solange referred to it as "relaxing creativity" and was certainly a fine way to pass many a winter's day into evening by our hearth. She chided me often over my basket overflowing with half-finished projects of embroidery and crewel. The planning of the projects and the initial coming together of them was where I found the pleasure. The feel of the vibrantly colored textures and varying hues of thread across my hands as it slipped in and out of my fingers and woven through fabric of silk, satin, and wool engrossed my senses and I could become lost in creating the initial form of a tapestry.

Once the colors and form began to take shape, and I could see the finished piece clearly in my mind's eye, the repetitiveness toward completion became boring and tedious. Each project Solange began she completed. Thinking it through thoroughly before she began and enjoying the process and detail of the work, each piece evolved into a lovely completed expression of herself. She might work on two or three pieces simultaneously but, unlike myself, no project she began was ever left to wait for an inspired hand to see it to completion.

Over a single change of seasons, pillow and chair covers, table runners and table cloths of various sizes were completed and placed in the large wooden box, and taken in late fall as donations to the charity Holiday bazaar. Our needlework was highly esteemed and we had eager patrons vying to purchase and asking for "just an early peek" at what we would be offering for sale each winter.

I often thought these loyal customers from year to year purchased our handiwork and presented them at the holidays to relatives who never knew the delicate and intricate artistry to come from any others hands than their own Dear Aunties or Grand-Mères.

My caustic comments always caused Solange to smile, but she never remarked other than to make me promise to complete a project of my choice at least every two months throughout the year. Choosing projects that required the fewest hours to complete, and thereby reducing the tediousness, I was able to discipline myself and contributed, if not equally to Solange's, considerably to our cache of finished items ready for donation and sale. My pieces were comprised of smaller items such as short table runners and small pillow coverings. These I could accomplish in a shorter amount of time and still make my every-two-month quota.

As I worked on these small pieces, I began experimenting with unique variations of color and texture. After some time, I became frustrated as I could not create with the fabric and thread what I envisioned in my mind. Solange often commented that she believed I had an "artistic bent" and that spring employed an old man to teach me drawing and watercolors. He smelled of mothballs and constantly had bits of pipe tobacco stuck in his salt and pepper moustache which completely covered his upper lip. He mumbled when he spoke and, able only to see a bottom lip, I often had no clue as to what he was saying. It soon became clear that his mumbles consisted primarily of comments about my "untraditional use of form and color". He seemed at a loss as to what to do with his atypical student. After Solange told him that he must persevere and, I am sure, increased his payment, he reluctantly introduced me to the medium of oil paints. Here I found what fulfilled my desire to create texture upon texture of vivid color and, form "went out the window with the devil", as my teacher so succinctly informed Solange.

The smell of the paint and turpentine thrilled me as well, but Papa insisted that I was filling the house with "unnatural odors". Solange relegated me to what had been a storage room on the second floor where I could create among the pungent fumes to my heart's content. This became my "studio" as I called it, and I loved the hours spent lost in this other world. No one referred to my "pieces", as I took to calling them, as art but this creative outlet filled me with an excitement and a sense of accomplishment that I had not previously experienced. I would later realize that Solange would support any endeavor that eased my restless spirit and kept me home.

I had found a long wooden table down at the wharf and talked a fisherman into selling it to me. Here I kept all my supplies laid out in a whirling array across the table top. The colors of my oils were vibrant and I most often used many-hued blues, ochre, yellows, scarlet and greens. The table top was smeared with these colors creating a canvas of its own. For the paintings I used white canvas stretched across small wooden frames, my "petite paintings" as Papa called them. Layer upon layer of color creating texture into which I often placed bits of thread or fabric. My studio began taking on a colorful life of its own as it began to fill with my paintings. Only the pieces were not hung on the walls but sat on the floor leaned up against the walls about the room.

Solange and I took to having our afternoon tea in this room as I would otherwise have skipped tea altogether. She had placed two stuffed chairs and a small round table in front of the adjoining windows where the afternoon light streamed in, playing off the colors of the canvases round the floor and filling the room with a swirling luminescence. After tea we would work together on our needlepoint, or she might, as I often chose instead to paint. When Solange's fingers tired she would sometimes walk the periphery of the room picking up a painting, holding it close and then as far out as her arms stretched. She would sometimes make a comment about the colors or what thoughts crossed her mind as she gazed at the piece. She sometimes stayed until time to begin the preparations for dinner as Papa seemed to invite guests more frequently than ever. I would emerge some time later as the afternoon light began to fade and ready myself for dinner as well. Each morning though would find me once again in my so-called studio.

Over time, my small pieces began to appear in nooks throughout our home. When Solange chose a piece to display, she would take it to a woodworker who formed a frame of her own design to complement the canvas. The frames always provided a subdued border for the flamboyant middles and these she would hang on a space of wall which she deemed suitable. I sometimes wondered if our traditionally styled and furnished home of neutral colors and dark woods was at odds with these unexpected bursts of vibrant colors. With time we came to feel my paintings and her frames added interest and a certain modern touch to the otherwise staid interior. Solange, always subtle and very correct, took care to truly tuck each surprise of color into spaces few people other than the three of us would likely encounter. When a visitor did happen onto such a surprise, the reactions were varied and curious. Solange and I would smile as Papa explained to the visitor that the "petite paintings" were my and Solange's creations and were they not truly unique and inspired? We came to love them more because we knew Papa did as well.

And now, here in Meuse, sat this large displaced sewing box Solange had left me. I had not ventured too close to it. Had not lifted its lid to explore the treasures I knew Solange had carefully selected to include. I felt she meant to tempt me toward picking up a sharp needle in anticipation of sliding a silky thread through its eye or perhaps persuaded by tubes of paint to feast my eyes on colors so bright I might not bear it.

Truth be told, my practical self had reminded me of late that I could really do with an apron or two. I often found myself beginning to wipe my hands down the front of my dress often lost in thought, only to realize I did not have on an apron. I actually had no aprons here in Meuse.

Here, when walking along my river or walking among the lavender, I would choose a pebble or stalk of flower and go to place them in pockets that were not there. And certainly I needed those pockets to gather my eggs and keep my clothes pins. Yes, I missed my aprons and my pockets.

So I did what I always did now when I was in need. I made a request of Henri asking him if it was possible to secure several meters of a plain muslin cloth from which I could make a few aprons. And as always, he exceeded my request, both to my amazement and often to my consternation. Within two weeks he presented me with a bolt of muslin. A traditional beige hued muslin with tan and brown flecks, tightly woven and of a thickness that would easily take a needle and still hold its shape. This bolt of fabric comprised at least 15 – 20 meters.

I suggested we cut off only what I needed for three aprons, approximately five meters, and then he could sell the remainder of the bolt. Surely there was a great demand for the material as it had been in short supply during and now after the war.

"Yes, a good plan Mademoiselle Marie but I have a better one where we both will profit! Since you asked me about the cloth for the aprons, I have mentioned here and there to the Madames on my route that I may, within a reasonable period of time, have aprons for them to purchase. They are now waiting with great anticipation to replace their old worn out garments with new. I supply the cloth and you make the aprons. I will sell them and we share the profit! Viola! A better plan!"

Henri must by now, I realized, have totally anticipated my reactions and unequivocally discounted the first words that proceeded from my mouth after he presented one of his grand schemes. Not one to disappoint and looking at him directly, I stated a firm if somewhat louder than intended "No, absolutely not!"

He just stood and patiently waited for me to list with all the logic I always tried to muster, the multiple reasons that this was not an idea I was interested in pursuing or needed to pursue. I was already trading eggs to barter and was able to purchase other items and food I needed. I was already busy enough, where would the supply of cloth and sewing items continue to come from, I didn't want to spend my time sewing, how did we know that with all that effort anyone would want to purchase aprons, and finally, I had never on my own made a complete apron before.

"Yes, yes, all good reasons I am sure", he said as he transferred the wide bolt of cloth from his arms to mine. It was heavier than I expected.

"Let us begin with five aprons then. Nothing too ambitious. The war is over and we must discard those things which harbor remnants of sadness and replace them with that which is new and full of hope. New aprons are just what a new day calls for! Oh, and be sure to cut a few to fit the wider girths of some of our more fortunately endowed Madames."

With that he climbed aboard the wagon, Donkey beginning to move slowly forward before he even released the reins from their hook. With what I hoped was a looked of great agitation, I abruptly turned and stomped toward my front door. I tried to ignore the feelings of anticipation as my eager fingertips ran lightly across the slightly grainy surface of the muslin I carried. First, before the thought of any others, I would make one apron and it would be mine.

Three days later, rain pounding loudly on the roof, I awoke early. The wind lashed the water hard against the windows and I recognized the quick hits of hail as well. A good day for staying indoors and without much to do, I felt snuggling down into my featherbed a better option than setting feet to cold wood floors. My second thought, that it would a good day to finally explore my sewing box, I attempted to push aside in lieu of more sleep. But the renewal of hail pounding on the window caused me to acknowledge that more sleep would not be possible. Still resisting, I dozed a little longer waking suddenly knowing the horse and chickens needed care, wood brought in and fires stoked. And besides, I was hungry. Eggs and tea might fortify me for my long-procrastinated reacquaintance with my sewing box.

The sense of fear I felt was certainly unreasonable yet very real. What could a sewing box harbor that caused me such trepidation? Animals fed, wood brought in and fires stoked, hours passed and I still had not ventured toward the sewing box. Finally at noon, carrying the box with me as I sat down on the floor, I slid the large heavy box toward my crossed legs. With a deep sigh I pushed the hook latch to the side and the box literally sprang open. How had Solange managed to fill it so full and still set the latch?

Lifting the lid fully open, my senses were immediately assaulted with memories. Not the sight of what was in the box but the smell. Smells evoking memories of home and family. This was the reason for my fear. Always acute to smells and the associations they called forth, I was overwhelmed with a longing for a time before. Before war and grief and loss rained down upon us all.

Every home I have ever entered was infused with the unique fragrance of that family and its domestic life. When I thought of friends left in Marseille, I could picture them clearly recalling the smell of each home with its particular piquant that might be made up of garlic and olive oil, fish or roast, scented candles burning in the foyer, the perfumes worn by those in residence and, occasionally, the family's dog would add to the bouquet.

My sewing box emitted the complex and familiar odors of wood polish, cloves and cinnamon, Papa's cherry pipe tobacco and

Solange's delicate perfume. I did not submit to any further hesitancy but eagerly lifted each item gently from its cramped quarters - unwinding or unfolding each lovely treasure, lifting it to my nose to smell, feeling the texture between my fingers and then laying each ribbon, floss of embroidery thread, skeins of yarn and spools of thread around me as I sat there on the floor. Soon I was encircled by reminders of my sister's love and generosity; her knowledge of what I would find fine and beautiful and would entice me toward awareness.

The early afternoon sun broke through the clouds setting the circle of color around me ablaze in shimmering colors so vivid I had to look away, my thankful heart I hoped transcending the distance to my family. The remaining hour of light I spent slowly exploring the remainder of sewing box. It was deep; deeper than I recalled but then Solange would have removed any items she felt I would not need or want, replacing them with others whole and new.

There in the very bottom was a long rectangular wooden box with a wrapped bundle tucked close beside it. I knew immediately the wooden box contained new oil paints. There were seven tubes in all and all my favorite colors; all the bright hues I so loved! The other wrapped bundle held a variety of brushes, a small palette, my paint knife and carving tool. Charcoal sticks and several lengths of colored chalk were there as well. My sister, my dear sister. The treasures she offered me within our sewing box I knew were tokens of acknowledgement. Her kindness contained within this box acknowledging again understanding and permission for me to carry on. I felt again our closeness; our sense of deep caring and love for one another and was again thankful for her visit in July. Tomorrow I would write to her expressing my appreciation. I felt remiss now that I had not opened our sewing box sooner so I could have written her of my gratitude. It would be a welcomed letter I was sure.

I had set bread to rise late that morning and rose now to place it in the oven. Out then through the back door to gather more wood to lay just inside the door against the wall. Out again to stroll around my home in this evening's last light needing to remove myself for a brief moment from the memories inside. I had had nothing to fear from my sewing box and its memories. Thankfulness and a deep sense of peace, which had with time become my abiding emotions here in my home in Meuse, were only deepened by the knowledge that my memories also included those of another home in what seemed another time, and those memories were welcomed here as well.

Walking back to the chicken coop and finding two warm eggs for my dinner (and again wishing for a pocket or two) and picking up two more pieces of wood for the stove, I paused at my back door before lifting the latch. Greeting me upon entering was the smell of baking bread, warm fires and lavender mingled with the lingering scents from my sewing box. This was the fragrance of my home.

Chapter 13 – Aprons, Fall 1921 – Winter 1921

Once a year Solange had us peruse all of our clothes deciding what we kept, needed to mend, and depending upon the fashion for the coming year, updated with a cut and stitch here and added lace there. Depending on our clothing allowance and Papa's plans for upcoming dinner soirées and the need for our appearances to reflect well on Papa's financial status, we sojourned two or three times a year to the shop of our favorite dressmaker. Not an event I ever looked forward to. I knew that Solange didn't especially enjoy spending hours looking at fabrics and discussing cuts and lengths, costs and so forth but, she did it with greater aplomb then I could ever muster. Sighs and groans were my occasional contributions to the swirling conversation surrounding the putting on and pulling off of muslin samples. The texture and colors of the fabric were of interest to me only and I chose those carefully often causing Solange to roll her eyes at my choices of colors bolder and textures more intricate then the current fashion would dictate. We would compromise when I was in a collaborative mood or the color choices uninteresting, always leaving Solange to decide the final cut and style of our garments.

We also had a variety of protective smocks for different garments and different occasions ranging from elaborate smocks over more formal dresses and made by the dressmaker of complimentary or matching fabric, to our clean well-worn comfortable smocks we wore over housedresses when alone at home.

Our aprons were not above the yearly inspection of to-keep or not-to-keep. We both had our worn favorites and, with the handling of each one, we would tell a snippet of story or remembrance. Remember when Monsieur Robart flung the leg of lamb at his wife just as dinner began and I mopped his wife's brow clean of the splatter with this apron? See the stains from the wine sauce still here? Oh yes, that apron was to be kept! Or the time Cook decided she would brew mead and it all exploded as it sat aging just behind the furnace. We were sitting at the kitchen table peeling potatoes when the explosions began and beer flew out from the furnace covering everything including us with its warm sticky dark liquid. We pulled our aprons over our heads and ran for cover! Giving up our aprons tied to such memorable stories or events were so difficult in fact, that we decided rather than to be rid of them, we would put them into a chest upstairs along with other items of memorabilia.

Elise was the seamstress who over the years had made our simple aprons and housedresses. She was now an elderly woman and had become a close friend. At least three times a year, Solange and I would choose and buy the fabrics for the garments and Elise would come to the house for tea and lunch and we would spend most of a day or two chatting and cutting patterns together. We had our favorite apron patterns and occasionally we would change a pocket size or number of pockets and modify the length or cut of the apron. Often I would add a bright spot of color chosen from my many scrapes of fabric. Over the many years, Elise's fingers stiffened and her eyesight faded. I began to do most of the cutting and Solange often the finishing stitches. Elise's only source of income was her sewing and she would remain our seamstress, if in name only, as long as she was able to come visit and bestow upon us her gracious good nature.

And now here I was in another time and place, in Meuse, completely alone with no Solange or Elise to direct and contemplating the making of aprons. Eyeing the waiting bolt of muslin Henry had procured for me, I took sketch paper from the sewing box and attempted to duplicate from memory the simple straight design; cut in one piece with added ties at the neck and waist. Narrow ties of muslin for the neck and a wider set of ties at the waist both attached to the finished edge of the body of the apron. Lifting again the lid of my sewing box I found my measuring tape and stretched the length of it from my collarbone to below my knee. One meter of muslin would do well for a single apron. The rhythmic sound of unrolling the heavy bolt across the wooden floor of my sitting room between the divan and the mahogany table, seemed loud in the quiet stillness of the morning. I measured one meter and cut straight across the muslin using a line of floorboard as a guide. My sharp cutting shears vibrated against the wood floor and up through my hand. Every sense seemed heightened; every stroke of the shears filled me with anticipation mingled with fear. How silly of me! I had been making aprons for as long as I could remember. Yes, but not alone, on a bare wooden floor with only the sewing box and vibrating shears for company, knowing that I would now be the seller of aprons rather than the buyer. This caused me to smile, let go of the fear and finish the straight cut.

Unfolding the cut fabric I smoothed out the center crease as best I could to check the straightness. I began to feel a remembered sense of eagerness and impatience. Always in my painting and sewing projects— maybe all aspects of life, I found not the final result, but the process of creating to be the most exhilarating!

Folding the length of the muslin together again, I picked a piece of drawing charcoal from the sewing box and proceeded to dot cutting lines marking a narrowing at the curve of underarm and bodice down to a tapering at the waist and widening again from hips to knee. Making fast work of cutting, shears moving swiftly across the wood floor through the muslin, I soon had my first apron cut. I then cut another apron keeping this first cutting as my original pattern.

The flat iron was heating on the stove top and a bowl of water lay on the kitchen block ready for sprinkling water for steam. Ironing first the seam into flatness, the scent of water on cloth as it met the hot iron sent a wave of memory as the steam swirled all around me. What a heavenly fragrance! Turning all the edges under wasn't as easy as I had hoped. And although I loved the aroma and the feel of hot cloth, the task took much longer than I found interesting.

Thankfully the muslin was thin enough to fold well and, as long as the iron was hot and the fabric damp, I was able to fold all edges into a hemline. Pinning as I went, it must have taken me well over an hour and several scourged fingers to hem half the apron. I bemoaned again my dark kitchen deciding that I would do cutting and ironing only on bright days when I could open the back kitchen door for the afternoon's light. But I had forgotten that I could open the shutters of the two closed kitchen windows. This I did and winter's light poured through those panes infusing my spirit and transforming my kitchen to a place of light. Now with a brighter workspace where I could see the fabric so much better, and the repetition of folding and pinning now familiar, the ironing under of the edges was soon completed.

Taking the still-warm apron into the sitting room where the light was also coming in from those windows, I sat on the floor beside my sewing box threading a new needle with muslin-colored thread. Easily done, I leaned against the wall toward the kitchen with light from all my windows and slipping my comfortable old thimble onto my index finger, I began to hem this first apron.

Before the sun was halfway round the house, the hemming was completed. Now I cut the neck and waist ties and would leave the ironing, hemming and attachment of those until tomorrow. With enough light left of the day, I cut out two more aprons and ties. Time had passed quickly and my stiff limbs and sore fingers confirmed that I had spent most of the day on just this first apron! Would it be worth these hours? I certainly needed to become faster than I was now if I was to profit from such an endeavor. But I did have to admit I found the time spent rewarding and even found myself humming from time to time. Certainly Solange would smile when I wrote to her of my sewing project.

Ten days had passed since Henri left the cloth in my arms. I knew he would pass again in another two or three. Did he really anticipate that I would have five aprons completed for him to take and sell? Stubborn as I was and working several hours each day, I completed each new apron in much less time than the one before. I had completed the five aprons. Of course I did! The first and most poorly put together apron would be mine. Henri could take the other four and do as he pleased.

There remained at least ten meters of muslin but I packed up the sewing box not wanting to begin more. What if they didn't sell? As a last thought, I had put a deep pocket onto the front of the five finished aprons. Surely these deep pockets would be a benefit to any woman as they always were to me.

As expected, Henri arrived two days later with talk of his latest acquisitions and what he had sold and to whom. I listened with few comments waiting for him to mention the aprons which he did not do. We exchanged eggs for goods and still he had not asked. I realized it was I who would bring up the topic and he would but wait. He made as though to leave when I finally told him I had four aprons which he could take to try and sell. I was wearing the first I had made as I am sure he noticed immediately upon his arrival.

"Oh good Mademoiselle! Are they identical sisters to the one you are wearing?" he asked.

"Yes", I said as I moved my hands up and down the front of the one I was wearing. "But the other four are better made."

"Turn around and let me have a look", he said twirling his fingers in the air as a cue for me to do the same. "Yes, they will do fine. Very fine Mademoiselle!"

I raced to the house returning with the four aprons neatly folded one on top of the other and quite ceremoniously laid them into Henri's arms.

"Do you really think anyone will buy them?" I asked.

"Yes! For I have already sold ten more. Sight unseen but greatly anticipated!" he said with dancing eyes.

With this last remark he turned toward the open end of the wagon, gently placed the finished aprons into a box, and turned back round producing a large stack of cut cotton swatches of various colors and sizes in many different prints. Folded like pieces of patchwork squares for quilts, the thick bundle was tied with twine and like the bolt of cloth, was heavier than I anticipated.

"Many of the ladies requested a little color and adornment to their aprons. Your well placed pockets would suit well for a little color, no?" And with that he was off once again. My aprons already sold and ten more to be made!

Next day and chores completed, the afternoon found me once again on the floor in my sitting room facing the windows untying the twine to set loose the stack of fabric patches. Most were folded into fours stacked again and again one upon the other. Unfolding the pieces, some were larger than others, some square and others rectangular measuring as large as an eight to a quarter of a meter and would be large enough for a separate bodice. The smaller pieces were certainly large enough for pockets. The fabric was all unused and obviously remnants from a dressmaker or seamstress's cuttings.

Close to the bottom of the pile, I found the largest piece of folded fabric measuring almost two meters. It was a pattern of delicate flowers of vibrant cornflower blue. Unfolding it over and over, I laid it out on the floor in front of me. There was enough of the lovely material surely for a simple dress.

Chapter 14 – The Pomegranate, Winter 1921

Everything about Henri is worn and dusty. His flopped hat, the brown hued pants and ever-worn jacket of indeterminate cloth must have covered him for many years as he traveled up and down these roads. His creaky wooden wagon, the metal hinges crusted with rust loudly announcing the opening of the wagon's rear portal to reveal hidden wares deemed necessary for the discriminate buyer, seemed also an extension of Henri's being. And Donkey, with no other name I knew or was ever heard uttered by Henri, was of an indeterminate age as well. With his left eye glazed over and most likely unseeing and both his long pointed ears notched and scarred, Donkey looked as though he had participated in fierce battles. How long had these two warriors of traveling commerce been together?

Now, if I allowed myself, hearing Henri's singing as he climbed the road from the north to my house, could possibly make me smile. I am hoping today he may have sugar. He is such a constant and possibly a reliable friend. Other than my infrequent trips to town with shopkeepers, he is my only contact with places beyond my own.

Donkey greets me this day with a turn of his head in my direction and graciously accepts my scratches and hugs to his warm neck. Henri watches us as he descends without a greeting and moves with seeming intent to the rear of the wagon quickly opening its door, preparing to set before me what he believes I desperately need.

The back of the wagon falls forward to form a flat table-top and today he lays but one item in the middle of this space. A large ripe pomegranate. One of the largest I have ever seen. Ripe with red color bursting from its skin. Henri looks away from this fruit to my face. He is serious today. Even his eyes that smile when all else is contemplative are today dark.

"Mademoiselle Marie. How are we today?" he asks.

"We are well", I say.

"Mon Dieu! Our winter is cold this year. How are your little chicks doing in this air?" he asks.

I hand him my basket of two dozen brown eggs and tell him the cold doesn't seem to affect their laying. He takes the basket of eggs and places them in the dark hold of the wagon.

"Fine, fine" he says impatiently as though the eggs are beside the point.

Although I am ever curious, I never ask Henri how far he travels north and south on this road; what towns he visits or where he acquires his goods. He is a pedlar, a gypsy-man I assume, and when I did once ask "how long he had been in commerce" his eyes smiled and he said, "It is the donkey that is in commerce and he just brings me along." I had not asked further. If he were so inclined, I imagine he would have many tales to tell.

Henri seems as private a person as I and yet my friend and sometimes, I sense, my benevolent protector. Although we are not related in any way by a shared past or common peoples, we seem connected closely in these recurring moments during his visits. He is solicitous and seems genuinely concerned regarding my benefit. This must be his nature with everyone otherwise his caring regard on my behalf would be a puzzlement.

Bringing my attention once again to the pomegranate atop the wagon lid, he asks, "Do you know what lies here before you Mademoiselle Marie?"

"Yes I do," I tell him.

"So you are familiar with this most exotic of fruit?" he asks again.

"My Papa would sometimes bring them home from his travels and my sister Solange would place them in a large bowl in the middle of our dining table," I tell him.

"Did your Papa explain that the pomegranate is feminine in form and nature?"

I certainly could not imagine Papa assigning gender to a fruit.

Henri quickly glanced up at me, waiting perhaps for me to ask how this fruit related to my gender. I was silent.

"Do you not see your image lying here before you? Lovely in color and design? The skin reflects the light and is not so tender as the color would suggest, but tough enough to protect what lies inside?" he went on quickly and his eyes focused only on the pomegranate.

"In such a healthy fruit, as you see here, you can determine that below this covering of skin is life, rich red and waiting to burst forth. With color, color! The heart of the feminine; full to overflowing!"

I had never heard such words from Henri and certainly never amassed in such excited allegory. I stared intently at the fruit.

Henri stopped here, sighed and lowered his head. Had he known such a woman? Loved such a woman? He always had a tale to tell of each of his wares he presented to me, but never with such passion bordering on an intimacy that caused us both to avoid each other's gaze.

Henri seemed in no hurry to resume his treatise and certainly neither did I. His purpose I could only ponder as we stood in the all-but-forgotten cold of the day. But purpose he always had.

He began again, talking quietly now. "This fruit is full because it was well tended. Otherwise would it not be thin and dry of skin and heart?"

"However, I bring today for you another of the fruit; it still needs tending with sun and time. Then it will become full as well. In time its color too will reflect health from skin to heart".

And with that Henri pulled from the recesses of his ancient wagon another pomegranate. Just as large as the first, but this second one hard and unripe, perhaps plucked or fallen early from the vine. The skin was still mostly green with blushes of red color just beginning to move across the flesh of the fruit. A fruit for another season.

This unripe fruit he picked up and looking into my eyes said, "This one is for you Mademoiselle. You have time to tend again".

He placed it with great care into my hands as though it was precious, delicate, and fragile.

He began to close up his wagon saying, "I leave now and will be two days south and then pass by here again in four days. By then you may have need of more than I can offer today".

With that he began walking down the road beside Donkey, leading the wagon forward on foot, never glancing back as I stood there holding the unripe fruit in my hands. I had forgotten to ask about the sugar, but would not have had I even remembered. I did not think his stopping today was to sell but to offer, for whatever reason, this fruit that lay cold and heavy in my hands. I watched until he and Donkey were little more than figments in my mind.

I learned of Henri the man through the tales he told of all things he presented for sale or barter. Every pot, utensil, strip of cloth and cutting of cheese came with a story. Not just a story, but a sage tale woven of life's sinew.

Did Henri talk such tales with each wagon stop? With each household along his way? He must have known every family and theirs, and their tales as well. I had shared no tales with Henri, but eagerly listened and welcomed his voice as it was often the only other one I heard outside of the one in my own head.

I turned and walked into my house. A pomegranate. What was I to do with it? And what was I to do with Henri's tale? The late afternoon sun filled the sitting room with light. I placed the fruit in the middle of the table not far from the window's warm pane. It looked forlorn. I took a piece of colored scrap and laid it beneath the pomegranate. I slowly paced back and forth from the kitchen through the front room thinking on Henri's strange words and looking at this odd addition to my space; hoping it would somehow thrive. It would remain here in this room in the sun's warmth where it might have the opportunity to truly ripen. It was all the tending I knew to give.

Chapter 15 – The Beehives, Late Spring 1922

The house was far too stuffy and the warm spring air outside too inviting not to take my stitching to the river. The sales of my aprons were going well and I spent some hours of most days attempting to keep ahead of the growing number of requests for my work. I took pride in the fact that I was spending time in useful labor from which I profited and in turn allowed me to become even less dependent on Papa's kind generosity.

As I closed my front door, a blanket tucked under one arm, I had just bent my head down checking my basket for all needed sewing items when I caught a glimpse of movement to my right – out in my lavender fields just south of where I was standing.

I looked again, shading my eyes from the sun to see with some surprise, Henri standing in the fields gesturing with wide flung arms moving as if to encompass all the land visible. He was fiercely animated in what appeared to be a one-sided conversation with a nun who was running her hands through the lavender stalks and nodding at whatever it was Henri was imparting. I had never been to the convent and had met none of the Sisters residing there. I assumed this was one of them now standing in my fields with Henri. But why in the world were either of them here?

As I stood watching in the shadow of the stoop, Henri stepped off to the side revealing four stacks of wooden boxes – three to a stack. Beehive boxes? Old and worn well, they sat almost hidden among the lavender sending the ever present bees fleeing from the now tamped down area. Tamped down I am sure by Henri as he sat the bee boxes securely on the ground. I knew the Sisters at the convent were bee keepers as Henri had introduced me to their delicious honey when I first began purchasing food items from him.

And then I realized what was happening. What scheme Henri was now concocting for my benefit. Of course! Beehives in my fields. Was I now expected to tend and nurture bees promoting the making of honey – lavender honey? Had not this thought occurred to me also - that the lavender nectar from these bees would be divine? But never had I entertained the thought of actual hives in my lavender! I did often wonder where these thousands of noisy buzzing bees flew to deposit their gatherings and create their honey.

I stood still and continued to watch the two figures in my field. What was I to do? I remained just outside the door on the stoop hidden from their view as they remained intent in their conversation. Taking a deep breath (or was it a sigh?) I stepped forward knowing Henri had been expecting me to appear. I was unaccustomed to seeing anyone standing in the middle of one of my lavender fields – much less a Sister from the convent.

With his arms still in flight over the fields, Henri motioned me over to where they were standing. I had never seen him so excited. I glanced back at the road and there was Henri's wagon with Donkey at its head. Donkey was intently watching his master as well. Perhaps Donkey had never seen his master exuding such excitement either! Henri was persuading, selling, coaxing and I was suddenly embarrassed that he would, without even consulting me, think of offering my land's use to a stranger. I left the porch and as I approached, I felt the rise of anger.

"Ah, Mademoiselle Marie! This is Sister Agnès, the prioress from our convent toward Verdun. Now that our brave Boys are home or gone from us, Sisters are able to take up their former tasks once again. Life resumes, no?"

This was one of the Sisters from the convent that also cared for the soldiers and who had found the families of my two Boys. I eased at this recognition as well as at the calming effect of her demeanor. She exuded respectfulness and reassurance. I realized that this idea did not originate with her but she had been willing to come with Henri to see what plan he devised. I felt she knew him as well as I did.

Sister met my eyes with a slight smile and what I perceived to be a shared empathy as if to say, "yes, our friend here is sometimes forward but only with the best of intentions." I looked for any sign of pity in her eyes but saw only a pleasant woman with a patient manner and sensed she understood my confused and flustered state.

"Let me explain Mademoiselle Marie," Sister Agnès began. "We at the convent, the other Sisters and myself, are apiarists - beekeepers. Our convent has maintained a small thriving business producing honey and wax for making candles. Henri has for some time carted our wares to customers and markets north and south of Verdun. People seem more eager than ever to sweeten their lives now that life has begun again. We believe the demand for our honey will grow faster than our limited hives can produce. Henri has told me many times that your fields of lavender are full of bees and he persuaded me to come have a look and a talk with you."

Looking again into my eyes with what I acknowledged was her knowing that this was an awkward first encounter for both Sister Agnès and myself, I nodded to her. Henri should have brought her first to my door; approached me first to talk of this. Henri knew, of course, what I would have said.

Henri was searching my face, I knew hoping to find my countenance restored to a modicum of calm indicating a willingness to listen further. I did not avert my gaze from Sister Agnès as I was not yet calm enough to trust whatever words I might speak to Henri.

Seeing my hesitation, Henri seized his opportunity. "I have been describing to the Sisters for some time the expanse of your lavender fields and how your abundance of bees is a most excellent opportunity for expansion of making exquisite honey. So Sister and I, with your assumed permission of course Mademoiselle Marie, brought 12 hives today. Just as an experiment to be sure, to see if your lively bees might take to a home close to their favorite nectar. And, if so, then voila! You and sister can strike a bargain as to how they might buy your honey adding to their varieties for sale and a profit for you as well!"

Henri knew I was feeling overwhelmed. He knew I was caught by surprise just as he understood I never would have agreed to the hives had he spoken to me ahead of time. He also knew I was polite and would not want to appear disrespectful to the Sister. He knew my need for propriety superseded my distress regarding his presumptuousness and caused me to hold my tongue.

Once again Henri interrupted these thoughts. "The bees will be no trouble to you Mademoiselle Marie!" The hives merely serve as an abode for your bees and a storehouse for their endeavors for which the Sisters will pay you a fair price. Am I not right Sister Agnès?"

Sister's kind eyes looked at me again and in a gentle voice asked if I had ever tasted lavender honey. No, I told her, but that I had often imagined that it would be delicious.

Sister laughed quietly and said, "I want to be there when you have the first taste of your honey. It will not disappoint you. Should the bees take to the hives and should you consent to engage with us, there will be honey to overflowing. The hives brought today have been cleaned and prepared for new colonies and we should know in a few weeks if your bees find them to their liking," she added.

"But why here," I asked, "such a distance from your convent?

"Your land is a little distance from us, yes, but your fields are wide reaching and the lavender very healthy. Your fields are more alive with bees than any I have seen over the years. Although we have active colonies at the convent, again, we have no hives dedicated to producing nectar from the lavender as your bees in these hives would do here. Truly, I hope, if the bees lodge in these hives, we might come to an agreement. And, yes, the lavender honey will be delicious." As she said these last words a wide smile of anticipated delight spread across her face just as my mouth began to water.

Henri interjected, "And the beauty is Mademoiselle Marie – no trouble for you! I can bring Sister again in two weeks to inspect the work of our busy friends. A good plan, no?"

We truly were standing in the midst of hectares of early blooming fragrant flowers inhabited by throngs of bees – thousands upon thousands of them, the air alive with their movement and humming. I watched them for a moment alight on one bloom and then on to the next. Twelve hives. How many of them could live in twelve hives? I realized I was already licking the honey from a comb that could be created here in my lavender.

"Would we really know in just two weeks if the bees take to the hives?" I asked.

Looking over the fields Sister Agnès replied, "Perhaps not as soon as two weeks but certainly by three or four. I would suggest we assess how things are getting along in three weeks' time.

"Alright," I agreed looking only at Sister Agnès, "let's proceed but I want to be involved every step of the way." I said emphatically.

I knew nothing about bees, hives or honey-making but I knew my land and my lavender and my bees had become a constant reminder of life moving around me and I found myself excited about this possible project.

Henri assured us both again that this would be a great success. His role, in addition to bringing Sister out for inspections, would be to transport the combs to and from my home in Meuse to the convent where the honey and wax would be extracted.

"And Henri," I asked finally looking at him, "What exactly will you gain from this enterprise?"

"Well of course," Henri concluded, "I will add the lavender honey to the other honey and bees wax candles already sold to customers both north and south Mademoiselle Marie. We all will benefit."

Although I found myself feeling excited I was still extremely exasperated with Henri but stubborn enough not to show him what I felt. Surely he realized he had overstepped the bounds of what would be regarded as appropriate intercession on my behalf and, without even my consent, regarding bringing these hives to my land? Henri's ideas and schemes always seemed, one by one, to cause me to take another step forward in life but, that in no way ever diminished my desire to want to chastise him severely for these intrusions into my affairs.

As we walked back toward the road and the waiting wagon, I asked Sister to explain how the bees might find the hives to their liking. She explained the hives they brought to my field were Langstroth hives and that several brood combs had been placed in the hives in hopes the nurse bees would nurture the larvae and create a new queen and then become active hives.

"Sister, I meant it when I said I want to be involved in all of it. I want to learn about my bees; about the honey. That must be part of our agreement."

"Of course Mademoiselle Marie. Sisters and I would like nothing more than to have someone new to teach. We become a little tired of ourselves and having a new friend to learn what we love would bring us great pleasure. If the hives are productive, we will talk together of adding more hives to your fields and we will certainly need all the help you can provide. With your permission, my Dear, I will come again, let's say in three weeks' time. Until then keep watch on the hives from a distance and perhaps you can see them begin to inspect their new homes. Hopefully they will find them to their liking. When we look together more closely in three weeks, we will begin our planning and your education". With a smile she placed a hand on my arm and turned to walk back toward Donkey and Henri's wagon.

I still did not meet Henri's gaze as he bid me a soft "adieu". Whether this was a fine idea or not, and that remained to be seen, he was not going to that easily be let loose of any guilt that might twinge across his mind over his impertinence.

Looking back at the hives, the bees were as always at this time of year, everywhere one could look. I would certainly keep a keen watch. As I watched Henri assist Sister Agnès onto the wagon seat, I couldn't help but think Henri was like Donkey, pulling a wagonload of potential on down a road to possibility.

Chapter 16 – The Other Sisters, May 1922 – Sep 1922

The bees quickly took to their new home in my lavender fields. When Sister Agnès, accompanied once again by Henri, came to visit the hives those three weeks after she and Henri first placed them in my fields, she announced with certain excitement that there was good evidence the bees were "settling in nicely". I felt Henri wanting me to meet his gaze but I was not ready for his gloating glare. I too was excited and glad that the bees were finding my lavender a worthy home site and felt a growing kinship with them. During those three weeks of waiting I had watched the activities of the bees closely. First silently observing from the side of the house and then gradually, as I saw them move in and out of the new hives, I found myself moving closer toward them. I also found myself humming along with their great buzzing hums and found they did not seem to mind my presence. I did not venture close enough to the hives to peer inside, but kept a ways back where the number of bees flying furiously to and from the hives were fewer. The constant sound of their activity however, could be heard as soon as I stepped outside my front or back door. They were comfortable companions and I was grateful for their music.

Sister Agnès came with Henri twice again in May. Sometimes I would see Henri between those visits and he and I would always walk out to the fields to check on the bees. He would venture close to the hives and seemed very much at ease with them. When I asked if he was ever afraid of being stung he laughed and said, "I have been stung so many times I no longer feel their barbs to my skin. I have helped the Sisters for several seasons now as they harvest the combs."

It was now the end of May and on Henri's and Sister Agnès's next visit they brought with them nine more hives. Sister brought with her wide brimmed hats with long netting attached all around and reaching nearly down to our knees. I wore long sleeved blouses when outside now and Henri had several visits ago brought me trousers which fit amazingly well. I always wondered what man wore them before Henri acquired them for me. I was going to ask him to find me another pair, as I was finding them so comfortable I wore them most every day! Dressed in our bee clothes, we completed a thorough inspection of the thriving hives to the south of my house and then placed the nine new hives in the fields to the back of my house. Sister Agnès was very confident that just as the first hives had done, other bees would quickly take up residence in these new hives. More bees, more honey and more music!

Now the beginning of June, Sister invited me to the convent to begin my "education in apiculture". Horse and I drove our buckboard wagon the hour plus, north on the road to the convent that next week. The day was warm and clear. It felt adventurous to be on my own with my own conveyance of horse and wagon setting off for somewhere I had never been. Other than the infrequent trips to town, there had been no reason for me to take any other excursions, and I truly welcomed the sense of freedom and change from my routines as I rode toward the convent.

Upon my arrival, the Sisters were so welcoming of me that at first I was overwhelmed by their enthusiasm, but not surprised as I felt we knew much of one another through the caring of the Boys and this new endeavor with the bees. Henri would certainly have communicated to them something of my situation.

This first visit to their home began with a tour of all the buildings and grounds comprising the convent; their house, their few outbuildings including a long narrow somewhat crooked and worn down shed, the herb, vegetable and flower gardens and the Honey House. The Honey House they saved for last showing me all the components and equipment needed for harvesting and processing the honey and beeswax. It was difficult to take it all in in one fell swoop of explanation. New terms and interesting contraptions were shown and their uses explained as the Sisters all talked over one another and sounded much to my ears like the humming of the bees in my fields. Moving back outside again, I asked if they kept chickens.

"Why would we do that Marie when Henri brings us fresh eggs from your hens?" Sister Béatrice replied with a gleam in her eye. I certainly knew I kept Henri well supplied with eggs and I was so happy to know that they arrived here and were actually eaten. I sometimes suspected that Henri took my eggs and aprons and never really sold them. I was further gratified, and rather proud, when Sister Jeanne, who was the resident cook for the convent, told me later that afternoon with our tea, how much she liked my aprons, especially the ones with the deep pockets. As I studied her features, I tried and failed to find some resemblance between her and my lost nurse-friend Jeanne and finding none I felt a sense of relief.

As Sisters and I spent ever more time together, our previously unspoken curiosities about one another began to find voices as we, at first cautiously, questioned one another about the small and few things we might have in common. They seemed to welcome as I did, someone besides themselves to talk with. I certainly had done quite enough talking with myself and cautiously relished the possibility of women friends again.

And what were the topics of these first conversations? Certainly the subject of Henri was common to us all! As we exchanged stories and anecdotes concerning Henri's involvement in our lives, we realized this man had affected us all and in ways that both amused and astounded. The Sisters all agreed he was "a God-send" and assailed me with examples of how after the war he appeared and found for them provisions when few were to be had. They had needed to flee quickly when war threatened their safety, and taking their apiary equipment when they fled to Belgium was never a possibility. When they returned to France, the Bishop found for them this piece of land; a former farm in need of repairs but generously donated by the landowner. With great gratitude, they were ready again to take up their cloistered life and their business with the bees. Henri procured for them much of the equipment including the hives and the extractor they needed to start anew. They in turn, supplied Henri with honey and wax that he sold and shipped to customers. I shared with them similar accounts of

Henri's coming to my aid and almost, but not completely and certainly not as readily, agreed that he was a God-send.

These stories of our mutual friend and benefactor allowed us time and, mingled with the opportunity to find cause for laughter, we examined one another and in doing so found an easy and compatible flow of give and take in our conversations. They cautiously inquired would I be offended if they asked me personal questions, admitting that they had long been curious about what brought me to my house in Meuse.

I felt a letting down of defenses; surprised that I was now ready and willing to open up to these women in whom I inherently began to trust. I felt a need to release some of what bound me so tightly; a wanting to be more at ease with living as I found them to be. I told them they could ask me whatever they wanted.

Their first question surprised me as I expected them to ask something personal regarding my experiences in the war, and I had mentally and emotionally prepared myself for what might prove difficult to answer. But instead they asked if I was ever afraid of living alone in my house on the river. I shared that I was thankful every day to my mother for leaving me this serene place of sanctuary. That on first arriving, the emptiness of the old house mirrored my own and I had immediately felt its willingness to take me in with no expectations. It had sat empty and aging long before I arrived, and was content to continue in the same state only now with an injured soul within its walls. I told them it was my sanctuary as much as I imagined their convent was to them.

They told me that none of them had ever lived alone and could not imagine being happy doing so. There were six Sisters at the convent and they had lived here together at the current site for the last two and a half years. They were extremely thankful for this lovely piece of land. They expressed the fear they felt as the war moved relentlessly toward them forcing their move to Belgium, and then again with the beginnings of persecution in that country. Throughout these experiences they remained together in one site or another as they had over the last twenty years. Remaining together, the six of them, despite the hardships of those war years and after, and strengthened by their solidarity and faith, they remained determined to return to France and re-establish their convent.

I found myself with tear-filled eyes nodding occasionally as they spoke, but chose not to share my own experiences during those same years of hardship. I supposed they knew I had been a battlefield nurse and because of my training and experience, they had Henri approach me on their behalf to take into my home and nurse the three Boys. I did not know if Henri had chosen to share with them the state in which he had found me when I first arrived in Meuse. I did know that they were appreciative of the care I provided to the Boys when they had no room for any more soldiers here at the small convent. Walking together over their grounds, we were silent for some time, all of us contemplating the memories of that horrid time of war. We were all, I thought, ready to move forward creating new experiences. I felt welcomed and, in turn, so grateful to be offered a place beside them.

In all my frequent visits over many years with the Sisters, talk of religion was never a conversational destination. I had never discussed my ambiguous Jewish heritage and they did not discuss their faith with me. It was obvious they were devout and their faith was in evidence in all they did.

Early on they shared they had all left the home of their parents between the ages of 16 and 18, moving into the family of the church and had been with other Sisters of their Order since that time. Other than their work in their gardens and with the bees, their routines centered on their prayers and chapel rituals, which to me, were somewhat mystical and fascinating. They seemed to hold *Le Vierge Marie*, The Virgin Mary, in high esteem. I saw evidence of their devotion to her in the few pictures in the convent chapel and in their frequent references to her in their everyday conversation. It was as though she was real to them. So real in fact that I often thought of Mary as another Sister. Unseen in the physical, but just as present.

Papa always made a point of instilling in Solange and myself a cautious attitude toward any outward display of religion. Finally after years of relentless asking, and when it was just the three of us at home on a Friday, we would sometimes observe Sabbath together in the privacy of our home. If Papa was to host a dinner on a Friday however, it was understood that no mention of Sabbath was ever to be spoken. We knew many of the men who attended the dinners in our home were also Jewish, but only talk of food and conversations both lively and serious ensued. Talk of religion – never.

Papa said we knew who we were and that was all that was needed. He instructed us to be wise and to never "add fuel to the fires of others' religious righteousness". Growing up I felt we three alone shared a well-kept secret. With the passing of my years, I have often thought that Papa was wise to be guarded. Even now at this time after the war, there were stirrings of religious persecution and I too, felt guarded when discussing any religious aspect of life. And, truth be told, I held little now in the way of faith - neither in my heart nor in my head. During that time of nursing in those killing fields, I was always just a prayer and a blasphemous curse away from God, accusing him daily of abandoning his own creation. The Sisters in contrast, seemed to wear their faith as a comforting shawl. It was never solemn, dark or secret. They seemed to harbor no anger at their God but only relief that he spared them from what could have been.

They each came to share with me their own personal stories of the circumstances surrounding their decision to become nuns. Sisters Marguerite and Jeanne shared they both came from very large impoverished families, and their parents easily made a decision early in their lives to "give" a daughter to the church. They were brought up knowing from a young age this was their destiny, but certainly never had a clear idea of the reality. They accepted the idealistic visions of devotion and piety fueled by their family and the Church.

Sister Evangeline said she easily and gratefully accepted her calling as she wanted to please her parents and ease the financial burden of having three daughters and no sons. I came to think of Sister Evangeline as the Garden Sister for she spent every moment apart from her religious duties out of doors in the gardens and dirt. She was never still and never happier than with a spade or rake in her hands.

Sister Béatrice, who never minced her words and could always provoke a laugh with her caustic humor and honesty shared, "From my earliest memories, I watched three generations of men beat and belittle the girls and women in our family. I had no reason to stay and every reason to leave. I had no use for men then and life has done little since to change my mind."

Sister Dominique confessed she cried for months upon arriving at the convent as a young girl, and her superiors came close to sending her home – a place she did not want to go back to. Growing up she had always wanted a husband and children and, by the age of 12 had a local farm boy all picked out. But she knew once her parents sent her to the convent there was no going home to her family as this would have been seen as a disgrace, and fear of her father's retribution soon dried her eyes. That explained her nurturing ways. She had found her family here, watching over the needs of her Sisters. She cared for the bruises, tended them when they were ill, made sure their garments were mended and consulted with Jeanne as to that week's food plan and what stores were needed. She was especially devoted to Sister Agnès.

Sister Agnès was their Prioress, the oldest Sister of the convent, and truly the center round which their lives revolved. Sister Agnès listened at least twice as much as she ever spoke. In all the times with the Sisters, when one of them voiced an opinion, brought forth an idea, or expressed an emotion, Sister Agnès seemed always to be totally engaged in whatever it was they wanted to impart. I wondered if this came with the responsibility for the care of her convent, or if it was her innate nature. I came to know it was the latter. She reminded me of a calm stately hen with her chicks. Sister Agnès seemed to always find ways to keep all of their minds sharp, their bodies busy, their conversations filled with laughter and their souls secure.

Through all the tales of how we all came to be where we were, Sister Agnès did not share what circumstances brought her to a life in the church. She seemed somehow above earthly considerations and, in my mind, was everything I imagined in a devoutly religious woman. She seemed to have a perpetual smile that reflected such a peace and harmony with all around her that I found myself wanting to always walk in her wake.

The Sisters were so different of personality, yet their overriding sense of devotion and love for this family they had created was their common bond. They were not only Sisters, but friends who enjoyed one another's company. Their harmony with the life they led and with one another extended toward me as well. I felt privileged to be so willingly included in their apiary work and their lives. They taught me as eagerly as I learned.

I remained curious in those first years of acquaintance as to what held them here in this place and to this simple life so grounded in faith. They said their devotion to *La Vierge Marie* and their prayers for her intercession for peace was their perpetual focus. All else they did, including their work with the bees and honey, were but secondary to their dedication to The Holy Mother.

I asked if they also revered the Pope in Rome. They laughed and said, "Of course", but Mary and Mother Agnès were their direct Superiors and it was obvious that was where their allegiance lay. They made me promise not to tell the Pope - or Mother Agnès! I loved their easy laughter; their way of looking at life seemed as simple as it was profound. I came to wonder if faith was the same as allegiance. If so then my allegiance would fall always to Papa and Solange. And sometimes perhaps with Henri if I was pushed on the matter.

My work with the Sisters in our endeavors to produce honey and candles fell into a comfortable pattern through late spring into late fall. Three days a week I would arrive at the convent at ten in the morning. I did not always need the wagon, especially once the combs were harvested, so just Horse and I made the trip. The Sisters would often be already at work when I arrived mid-morning and I would seamlessly join in. We would labor until one o'clock, take a meal together in their small dining room followed by a walk around the grounds discussing the hives and our tasks yet to be done, ending back at the Honey House to finish our work. Often when the weather of late spring, summer and into the fall would be warm and inviting, we would move the long table out of doors into the shade of the Honey House licking labels and sticking them to the fresh jars of honey and boxes of beeswax candles. Regardless of the season, I would always allow two hours of last daylight for my trips home again and, smelling of honey, wax and sweat, I would give Horse his head and we traveled to home.

As late summer settled upon us and the harried work of bee season gradually slowed, my visits became weekly and then by the beginning of September settled into twice a month. Our visits over the winter, when the weather allowed me to travel the roads, were more social as the gathering and processing of the honey was mostly completed. We still had much wax, and would continue making candles well into the early winter. We also tended to the cleaning of hives, readying them for the spring.

At the end of our afternoons of work, the Sisters never failed to invite me to afternoon vespers in their chapel, and I never failed to decline. While I accepted what they shared regarding their faith as their reality and knew their devotion to be sincere, I never felt any desire or compulsion to join with them in any religious ritual and they, respectfully, always made clear that would never be a condition regarding our friendship. I knew they continually extended upon me acts of kindness and I was beyond grateful. I knew they truly came to love me as I did them.

I would always take my leave with hugs all around. As I traveled home, content with the work we accomplished and with a renewed sense of community among these women, I was always filled with their reflection of peace and contentment. Over the years working side by side with these precious Sisters, peace and contentment gradually became my own reflection as well.

Chapter 17 – Fishing, May 1922

Stepping out the back door while still pushing sleep from my eyes and tugging my hair away from my face to find my way to the pump, the braying of Donkey quickened me fully awake. It was 6am. What was Henri doing here just after light? Walking around to the front of the house, Donkey let out a louder welcoming bray. Henri was nowhere in sight. Even this early, the morning summer sun was beginning to warm Donkey's grey back. My cool hands welcomed his warmth as I nuzzled closer into his neck. Where is your Master Donkey?

As if on cue, Henri's rich voice broke into song. Donkey and I both looked toward the river bank. My first thought was Henri must be bathing and I needed to stay put. My second, that I had seen more than one naked man in my life and Henri would have to take his chances, got the better of me. With one last warm hug from Donkey, I walked across the narrow road onto the gentle grassy slope looking down toward the river in the direction of the music.

Henri was standing on the bank throwing a string back and forth across the glistening water. Small bugs were hovering just at the surface and only momentarily scattered as Henri's line settled across the surface in one long straight line. Henri was fishing!

I walked down the slightly sloped bank approaching to his left. The new sun felt increasingly warm and welcome on my face. Walking up to Henri I saw there were four fish on the bank laid out neatly in a row.

With no apparent glance in my direction, he called a hearty "Bonjour Mademoiselle! Here we have a breakfast ready for cooking! One more lovely trout, then I fillet and we fry in cornmeal and have a feast!" I had not had fresh fish since Marseille!

This late May morning was pristine; cloudless and still, the sun's rising sending bright rays between the poplars illuminating all around in striations of light. My breath caught at the realization that in this moment I was welcome both of the company and the brilliant light which was seeping into my senses.

"You, Mademoiselle, hold the line now and catch our last fish. I will begin to clean the others. My ravenous hunger will make my blade glide through these scaly beasts. Make certain this last catch is long and fat!"

I still had not spoken. As I held this moment I wondered perhaps if I was truly awake. I took the line from Henri, wrapped it round and round my hand, and as he had done, held it still over the water. Henry hummed as he cleaned the fish and I had become lost in the river's mesmerizing flow when I felt a strong tug on the line.

"Henri! What do I do now?" I asked loudly struggling to keep the line secured round my hand.

"Pull slowly and continue wrapping the string around your hand. Hold it taut! Any slack and our brave sea beast will seize his chance to throw your hook!"

Our brave beast did indeed seize his moment and began jumping high in the air for freedom. With each wild splash the scales caught the sun's rays as again and again the fish jumped and twisted, tightening the line around my hand until it was biting sharply into my skin. I was not about to lose our breakfast and continued winding the line steadily moving the fish toward shore.

"Bien Mademoiselle!" Henri yelled as the fish made one final leap and flopped to the shore beside my feet.

I had caught a fish! There were fish in my river Meuse! Breakfast, lunch and dinner fish!

"Mademoiselle Marie, bring me your superb catch and I will teach to you the fine art of filleting."

Bending down to pick up my catch, it flopped in my hand hold causing me to startle with a loud gasp.

"Ha ha! Your fish will be the most flavorful as it is the most lively. Use your two hands to scoop it up and toss it here", instructed Henri.

I scooped and tossed, and Henri caught the slippery body as though it was dry and smooth. Walking to where he stood, I gathered his already cut fillets placing then into my deep apron pocket as Henri finished the last two halves placing them also into the apron. Gathering the fish carcasses, he tossed all but that of my catch into the river.

"Look Mademoiselle! Your fish was indeed full of life! She had many eggs inside her belly". I felt a momentary heart pang of regret as we turned and walked up the bank to my house.

"Off to find skillets!" exclaimed Henri as he walked ahead with great purpose. "You do have two cast iron skillets do you not Mademoiselle Marie?

Yes, I reminded him. They came with the provisions he brought before the men arrived. What I didn't say was I had not used them since the men had gone. Another pang at my heart. I picked up my pace to outdistance any pain and caught up to Henri.

"Did you build the fire up this morning Mademoiselle Marie? We need the stove hot for frying." I was glad to tell Henri that before I left the house, I placed several pieces of wood onto the still glowing embers of the stove. My mouth was beginning to water as my stomach rumbled, voicing its eagerness to eat!

"And of course we need two eggs from your coop and two potatoes peeled and chopped. I brought the bread crumbs and the cream for batter," he said as he jaunted to the wagon and I climbed the steps into my house to stoke the fire. I realized that his fishing this morning had not been a spontaneous occurrence, but a planned event. I felt the familiar twinge of caution and wondered what Henri was up to now.

Henri carried in the cream and crumbs where he found the eggs waiting on the counter. He quickly grabbed a stone bowl from the open shelf cracking the eggs and whipping the cream into a frenzy. I assumed he must be fueled by hunger!

I found the long-abandoned cast iron skillets and surreptitiously wiped away the thin coat of rust with a rag I had found. As I tossed a few more pieces of wood onto the bright embers, I placed the skillets atop the kitchen stove now flaming back to life. I quickly peeled and chopped the potatoes.

"Your lard please Mademoiselle Marie. Three tablespoons in each skillet." Henri instructed again. The lard crackled as it hit the bottom of the hot pans. When the lard was deemed hot enough to fry, Henri instructed me to lay the diced potatoes evenly in one pan as he laid the battered and crumb-covered fish in the other. I feasted on the aroma alone!

I was glad now for the mahogany table and chairs to hold our feast and make us comfortable while we ate! I hurried to clear the table of my sewing paraphernalia and as I stepped back into the kitchen, Henri lifted out the first batch of fish; five golden brown fillets. These pieces he set onto a cloth to drain and placed the last five into the skillet. He had stirred the potatoes and they were beginning to golden as well.

As I reached up taking two plates down from the shelf, he asked if I had wine goblets. "No", I laughed, "why ever would I have need of those?"

"Then any glasses will do as I have also brought a lovely white wine, a baguette and an aged camembert for desert. Take out the last of the fish and dish the potatoes Mademoiselle, and I will shortly return to eat," he said as he hurried out the front door. Hmmm. Again I wondered why he had gone to such trouble for a breakfast of fish.

Laying the last of the golden fillets on paper to drain, I divided the potatoes onto our plates adding to each five fillets. Grabbing two forks and limen cloths for *serviettes*, I all but ran to the table ready to begin eating as quickly as possible. Sitting at each place sat crystal goblets filled with a clear wine. In the middle of the table Henri had placed the small round of camembert and what looked like a fresh baguette. Where oh where did he find such treasures? It was a feast for the eyes as well as the palate. Besides my sister, this was the first meal in my home with a friend. Henri had never been inside my house other than when carrying up the beds, mattresses, linens and the Boys. He seemed perfectly at ease and at home sitting there in the sun filled room.

As the fish approached our greedy mouths, Henri quickly thanked the brave sea beasts for their "noble sacrifice". Had I ever tasted food this delicious? Fish this succulent and *pommes frites* so perfectly crisp? It wasn't until we began to break the baguette that we uttered sounds other than those of communal delight. Our mutual "ahhhs" and "ummms" indicated we agreed our feast was "magnifique"!

With a second glass of wine, camembert and a peach produced from who-knows-where, I shared with Henri my memories of shopping for seafood in the harbor markets along the wharf in Marseille. Solange especially loved octopus and would often buy it fresh from the fishermen as they entered the harbor and before they ever stepped ashore from their boat. She sliced it thin sautéing the opaque pieces in hot olive oil then drizzled with lemon and salt. Scallops and thick succulent white fish were often served from our dinner table to Papa's business guests. Solange only made the octopus when it was just the three of us as she said it had to be eaten hot from the pan. Henri listened attentively to my tales asking few questions but obviously enjoying the stories. He said he had all his life lived inland, always by a river, but never on the sea.

He asked if I missed living by the sea and my family in Marseille. I told him this home in Meuse provided the sanctuary I had needed and although I greatly missed my sister and Papa, I had grown to love the peace here in these last two years. This was truly my home now and I had no urge to return either to the city or the sea. I did love that the water and the river so near provided an additional peace and serenity that met my needs.

Henri sighed deeply, looked down and placed his hands on his lap. He then turned his head to the left, looked up and out the window.

"I knew your mother Marie," he said quietly.

My mind took a moment to catch what I thought Henri had just said. He knew my mother? I must have spoken this aloud as he said, "Yes, I was acquainted with your mother's family for many years Marie."

My hands had dropped lifelessly into my lap, the fish forgotten and the bread sitting just below my swallow. I swallowed again and again to keep it there as my heart raced and my mind filled with questions.

"How did you know her?" I finally asked.

Henri then turned back toward me and taking a long breath said, "She was twelve when I first saw her. Older than me by two years. I have travelled these same roads since I was quite young. That summer, I was travelling with my uncle."

Wanting to ask only about my mother but not knowing how, I asked what first sprang to mind. "Where were your parents Henri?"

"Oh, they were here – close by. My family was very large and comprised of many uncles and cousins farming on small parcels of land around our village. Between the planting and the harvest time, and usually two men together, we would traverse the roads to the outlying villages selling and procuring goods we bought in the larger towns. That way the families were kept together by the business as well as the farming and supplemented the meager incomes from the harvests. My father started to take me on the roads with him when I was seven. But even at that age, I was in conflict with him continually. As I grew into eight and nine years, we argued fiercely – about anything and everything. I always said I knew better and he always believed he knew best."

Henri stopped again, wiped his mouth on the linen and picked up his story. "By my ninth year, my father relegated me to travelling with my uncle who also had his own wagon and donkey. My father and I were both relieved at this new arrangement and our relationship improved the less we saw of one another. My father would take his wagon south and Uncle had this northern route travelling toward Verdun. That is why I missed those earlier summers of seeing your mother."

"My uncle was father's younger brother, but you would have thought them no relation. Uncle called himself "Pedro", which was a ridiculous name for a Jew. He said it sounded exotic. This was the only common opinion that my father and I ever shared. We both refused to call him anything but Uncle." Henri paused here and I followed his movement as we both took a drink of the wine.

"Uncle was full of mirth and, I often thought, too familiar with the customers. But he liked people and was interested in the lives of the families he sold to. My father, who was the eldest, was in contrast all seriousness. I realized much later that my father was perhaps never far from worry as he shouldered all the financial responsibility for the success or failure of the families. But I have ventured away from the story of your Maman." He said looking at me directly for the first time since he started his tale.

"So the summer of my tenth year, as we approached this house, I saw your mother and your own uncle. Actually I heard them laughing and singing before they came into view. This certainly caught our attention and my interest! The only person we ever stopped and sold to here was an older woman and I seldom took any notice of her at all".

"But these children were a different matter altogether! I wanted to jump from that bumpy wagon seat and ease my aching body and dust-filled eyes with the vision of them and run and run as they were. Actually only one was running. As we came closer, I saw the boy was seated on the ground laughing but joined in the song as the girl ran around and around him."

"Uncle called out a greeting and the children stopped their game and came toward the road to await our wagon. He knew their names: Edith and Paul. The children called him Pedro. How I hated that name but coming from them it seemed not half so bad. Uncle introduced us all and while the boy appeared shy, the girl was lively and full of questions. Why was I with Pedro today? How old was I? Did I go to school? What did we have in the wagon that they might like?"

"I had no answers for I had no thoughts. She filled all the air with her energy and I could not breathe. She was darting now all about the wagon and I wanted but to hold her in one place and put the pieces of her together."

"Her mother, your grandmother, came out of the house just then and proceeded to the wagon. She and Uncle conducted business as the other three of us conducted our awkward first business as well. For is it not the business of children to engage in play and inquiry? We stood in front of the wagon as far from the adults as possible. Uncle always talked loudly and when he was coaxing to sell, his voice took on a powerful timbre. He was in his element and was also a distraction as we three were attempting to scrutinize one another and conduct our own coaxing toward possible friendship."

"Your mother and uncle were dressed in simple summer frocks. She wore a blue flower print cotton dress with a matching cornflower blue wide satin ribbon at her waist and another of the same to hold her long blonde waves away from her face. Her skirt stopped just above her ankles and although she was now standing still, the toes of her bare feet were curling and uncurling as though standing in place was indeed a most difficult task. Her eyes, so like yours, were never the same color. Over the next three years of summer visits, we came I think, to know each other well. But what did that ten year old boy truly know other than the hope of desired friendship from someone so……...alive." He paused again looking at me with something much like confusion in his eyes.

"Our route took us north one week and then back south again the next with several days between at home with our families. I lived for those stops at your great-grandmother's house. This house. Your home now. For your mother was always either out of doors or, seemed have sense our coming, as she was always there at the front as though waiting. Perhaps our stops provided her with needed diversion from those long summer days with only a somber younger brother and two women for company. I dared not believe she looked forward to our stopping for my sake. She was all life and beauty, and I rode atop an old wagon pulled by an ancient donkey with my crazy Uncle Pedro."

"The long spance of those summer-to-fall months allowed me time to ever ponder the color of her eyes. Every spring I vowed that this summer was the one I would discern the true color and hold it fast in my mind's eye. Over three summers of visiting as we stopped here for as long as I could stretch each time, I never did determined their color."

"That last summer your mother and great-grandmother came alone. The hard cold weather of the previous winter had been too much for your delicate uncle Paul, and he passed just after the holidays of winter. Your mother was quieter, but her bare toes still danced and by the last of the August days, just before they returned home to Belgium, she was again, my joyful friend."

Looking again out the window Henri continued in a hushed voice that spoke of loss. "That was the last I saw her. Your great-grandmother continued for some years to come here to her summer home, but Edith never visited again. I begged Uncle to ask the grandmother for information. He told me it was out of the question. That it was none of our business. This struck me at the time as ridiculous as Uncle was ever curious about the comings and goings of everyone. I sensed he felt the loss as well. One summer, two years after her last visit as Uncle was closing the wagon, I found the courage to ask your great-grandmother after Edith. She remarked that Edith was now a young woman, and that her attentions needed to be focused on her future and carefree summers were a thing of childhood and in the past. She seemed to be reciting what she had been told, and knew she was lonely for her family."

"When you told me that this was your mother's home, I immediately knew you to be Edith's daughter. Your eyes you know. They change as hers did. And your chin, and your hair…" Henri looked toward me now again, and we both sat still looking intensely at each other across the table.

The sun was now mid-line to the poplars across the road. Hours had passed as Henri had transported us back in time. We were both fatigued. He from the effort of talking and myself from the mingled pain and joy of listening. I wanted details. To know her face, how her laugh sounded, the way she spoke and danced. I wanted to feel her arms around me. Details would have to wait. It had been a day of mixed and many blessings and all I wanted now was to think alone on what Henri had told me.

As we cleared the table I told Henri that no pictures or resemblances of any kind existed of either my mother or Solange's. That I had so often tried to conjure a picture of her in my mind. That I so appreciated his sharing his recollections with me. He lowered his eyes and nodded. There would be more opportunities to share once the talk of this day had settled in.

When Papa first told me about Maman's house in Meuse, he said that she had spent her childhood summers here with her grandmother. As Henri set about to leave, he answered my last question of the day confirming that although the house had been unoccupied for the last 20 years or more, he had kept watch on the property and often fished the river in the spring and summer as he did today. He checked for vagabonds and rodents making such repairs as might be needed and sometimes slept in the lean to. I realized then why the house was in such good repair when I arrived. Even in my initial state of depression and grief during those early months here, I had thought it remarkable that a house long abandoned had withstood the elements of weather and time so well over all those years. And now I knew why. And now I understood the source of Henri's fathomless wellspring of kindness toward me.

In my daydreams I had thought of my mother here as a grown woman, but never as a child. Why I don't know, as she had married my father at the age of nineteen and I was born one year later. And then she was gone. I wandered through my home those next few days trying to conjure visions of Maman, my grandmother, my great-grandmother and my little uncle Paul here at this same time of year. Outside I could picture them running and singing as Henri had described. Her in the blue flowered dress laughing and singing among the lavender.

And my grandmother. I sensed that I was perhaps more like her. I had a passionate nature and when riled I could respond too quickly with a comment or word. At those times, and with some humor I did not always appreciate, Papa would tell me I reminded him of my *Grand-mere*. No one would have ever describe me as "joyful" as Henri had described my Maman. I had always sought solitude and peace, now more so than ever – there was happiness enough in that.

Sitting on my steps at sunset watching the spring sun glide down behind the poplars into the river, I felt the presence of my family here with me. Even during the terrible time of anguish toward healing, they had been part of the solace here in my house in Meuse. My Maman had given me life again.

I sighed deeply, a smile coming to my lips, for when I looked down at my bare feet, my toes were dancing.

Chapter 18 – Pedro, The Little Beast, Sept. 1922

The rain fell fast and hard that morning. The torrents of water on my roof obliterated the welcome braying of Donkey and it wasn't until I heard Henri's loud callings of, "Marie, Marie, it is wet out here! Come give me your eggs!" that I grabbed my basket, covered my head, and ran out my front door and down my steps to the wagon waiting in the road.

Henri was covered by a large hooded poncho and as the rain began to let up, he allowed the hood to fall onto his back, his floppy hat still securely in place atop his head. He moved swiftly anticipating the clouds opening upon us again and he, more quickly, opened the back of his wagon. I handed over my full basket of eggs and seven more aprons and as he placed them deep into the recesses of the wagon away from the rain, a small animal emerged crying loudly.

"Ah!" Henri exclaimed in surprise. "Not you once again my little beast! How is it you always manage to find a ride?" The kitten was mewing loudly while his head nuzzled Henri's hand.

This beast was the smallest kitten I had ever seen. It was completely black but for white paws too big for his scrawny small self, and one ear was all white as well. I was very familiar with cats, as the port at Marseille was home to throngs of the stray animals and were constant citizens of the streets and markets. Cats were the rat-eaters and kept the ports' population of such rodents down to a manageable level, while all the while the good people of town pretended the rats were not existent. I had a visceral intense dislike of rats and saw cats as a necessity to be tolerated.

"Yes, yes, little fellow. I will feed you momentarily," Henri said handing me the now purring black kitten. "Please hold him Marie and I will find him some nourishment".

Taking the warm kitten, I gathered him to my chest to keep him at least partially dry from the now sporadic fall of rain drops. He crawled upward and settled into the curve of my neck and began to purr more loudly. I felt instantly warmer. As Henri laid some small cut up pieces of smoked fish out on the table of the wagon front, I attempted to place the kitten there as well to eat. But the little fellow was having none of it and his small sharp claws extended with my continued attempts to lift him from my neck. I gave up trying to coax him off of me (the claws were quite a deterrent) and I succumbed to his clinging to the fabric of my dress as he settled once again into my neck, continuing his music of contentment.

"Henri, can you please help me dislodge your cat from myself so he can eat?" I asked.

"He is not my cat Marie. He is nothing but an escapee from his litter mates. A smart one he is for he has done this before knowing I will not let him starve and thus he scampers up inside the wagon when I am loading or unloading. Just let him rest where he is. He must need your warmth more than my food."

Henri proceeded to find me my requested bread, tea and sugar from the wagon and after laying these goods up again by my front door out of the rain, came once again to the wagon. He quickly closed up the back and proceeded, with what seemed a hasty retreat from what I assumed was the increasing rainfall, to jump aboard his wagon and make as though ready to depart.

"Henri, you are not leaving this cat with me! I am serious Henri!" I said realizing his intentions.

"It is not I that am leaving the cat Marie, but that the cat has decided to stay!" And with that he lifted the poncho's hood back onto his head over his hat, told Donkey to go forward and off they went. He did not even leave me the dried fish to feed this little beast!

Oh well. It was not such trouble. I walked toward my house with the warm sleeping kitten tucked deep into the recesses of my neck. It would not wake or be woken even when I stooped to retrieve my food supplies from the porch stoop. With one hand I held the kitten securely, and with the other made two more trips to and from the door to take and put away the goods. Again the kitten began to purr. I felt the sound through my body and knew he was mine. Pedro. I would call my *petite* beast Pedro.

Chapter 19 – Healing, Late November 1922

It was barely light on what I believed to be a Monday morning, when I heard loud knocking at my front door. My door had never received a knock during my time here and it caused me to jump and move quickly to the front window to see who might be standing before my door.

It looked like Henri but not quite. What was he doing here this early and why was he knocking so urgently at my door? I hastily wrapped a shawl about my uncovered shoulders and moved to unbolt and open the door.

"Dieu Merci Marie that you are up and about! I apologize in the extreme that I must seek you out so early but am most glad you are available."

He was standing with his hat held before him in both hands and turning the edges of the brim round and round with his fingertips as he spoke. It was evident he was in great distress. My first thought was of Donkey and my second thought was, having only seen Henri without his hat perched on top his head once before, how Henri's dark hair was very thick and quite lovely. Long at the sides and tucked back behind his ears, the glossy dark waves rolling over his head, for whatever reason, had caught me by surprise. He looked almost young standing there in the early morning light.

Bringing myself back to his urgency, I asked, "Henri, has something happened to Donkey? Or you? What's wrong?"

"No, no Marie. Donkey and I are fine but it is Sister Agnès. I have hurried here from the convent to bring you to them. They bid you come quickly as Sister is in great need of your healing." Henri accompanied these words with gestures toward Donkey and the wagon.

"What do you mean 'my healing' Henri? What's happened to Sister Agnès?"

"She has fallen with a great gash to her head. The Sisters have stopped the bleeding but Sister Agnès has a wide wound and has not awaken from a sleep. Please Marie, let's go now, quickly."

"Yes, yes Henri. Give me just a few minutes to gather some things."

Things? What things would I gather as I had no true medical supplies? Thinking quickly I grabbed strips of muslin from a basket of material scraps. From my sewing box I quickly took my small scissors, three needles of different sizes and two spools of my heaviest thread. Placing these in a cloth bag and hurrying into my cloak as I walked out the door, I found Henri waiting with reins in hand atop the wagon.

He pulled me swiftly up by my empty hand and as I sat down beside him I asked, "What do you mean she is sleeping?"

"I have not seen the good Sister as when I arrived at the Convent, Sisters Dominique and Evangeline were waiting with this news and then hurried me off to go for you."

What I wondered during that ride to the convent was whether Sister Agnès fell first and suffered an injury to her head that caused, hopefully, just a temporary loss of consciousness or did she suffer a more serious event previous to the fall? In any case I knew I could at least conduct an examination and suture the wound. Although my medical training and battlefield experience with trauma and injury might allow me to treat her superficially, I was not a physician and skills much greater than mine might be needed.

"Henri, why did you not go to the local physician the Sisters would call upon?" I asked.

"He left at the beginning of the war and has not returned. He was a single gentleman and joined the ranks of the medical corps early on in the war. No one has had word from him; if he survived and if so, if he might return. Hence the need for your services Marie"

"You do know Henri that I am a nurse and not a physician."

"Why yes of course! We all know that you are an experienced nurse and a gifted healer. Did you not heal the Boys and return them to their families? The last letter received at the Convent from their family joyously reports their continued improvement and is a testament to your skills!"

Inwardly I groaned and feared another expectation, a greater expectation, was being placed on me once again. But at least in this situation I had the security of training, experience and some success. I was terribly worried for our dear friend and knew I must, for the remainder of the bumpy ride, set my mind to putting on my nurse's mantle in preparation to deal with her needs apart from my emotions.

Henri and I rode the remainder of the ride with our own thoughts. As we approached the convent and I shaded my eyes from the sun's rising, as silhouettes of three Sisters appeared from yet a distance away. As we neared the convent they began moving toward us with cries of, "Hurry, hurry!" and "Merci mon Dieu! You've come!"

I rushed past their confidence, jumping from the wagon with my bag of hope as they gathered me into them and moved us inside to Sister Agnès's room. I had not been to the Mother Superior's room before but it appeared much the same as the other Sisters' rooms. Small and spare. This room, however, faced the east and the morning sun streamed through the window beside the bed on which Sister Agnès lay. She was illuminated in this light and I could not help attributing some meaning to her shining countenance. Whether a positive or worrisome portent I could not yet know.

Henri had told me Sister Evangeline had been in constant attendance at Sister Agnès's bedside and now she motioned me into the chair beside hers. We were all silent as we sat or stood about Sister Agnès for those first few moments after my arrival. My initial observations, as I saw her face sustained some color, allowed me to exhale with relief and confidence that she was not at death's door. Her chest rose and fell gently and as I placed my index and middle fingers to her neck, I found the pulse strong if somewhat erratic. Turning next to exam her wound, I found the gash on the left side of her forehead was at least 1½ cm deep and 5 cm in length. It was red raw and gaping, but clean and not bleeding. The Sisters had certainly done well in taking good care of their Prioress and friend. I attempted to wake Sister with a gentle shake, calling her name quietly and then more loudly with more fervent shaking and rubbing of her hands. No response.

"Please tell me what happened, how long ago and what caused this gash to her head?" I asked the other Sisters gently.

"We were in the garden yesterday afternoon, picking the last of the tomatoes and decided to pull up the dead vines. But it's been so dry and the ground was so hard, Sister decided we needed the shovel from the shed as we couldn't pull the vines cleanly from the ground", Sister Evangeline explained.

"I went on with the picking for some minutes and then paused as Sister Agnès had not yet returned with the shovel and we had not much time before Vespers. She wasn't walking back from the shed and I wondered if the shovel had been misplaced and she couldn't find it. Had I maybe laid it somewhere out of sight?" Sister Evangeline paused and stilled herself before continuing.

"I decided to walk to the shed thinking I could help her find the shovel. I didn't see her when I first walked in. The tools are kept at the far end of the shed and it was walking that way that I saw her. She had fallen to the ground and lay on her left side, the cut side of her head on the dirt floor. She wasn't moving, and as I knelt beside her I saw the blood. It was still running onto the ground. I ran as fast as I could for help." Near tears and visibly shaken, Sister Evangeline paused in her story once more. I rose and guided her gently by the elbow to a chair where she could sit and compose herself.

Sister Dominique picked up the story from there. "After initially trying to rouse her in the shed and finding we could not, we raised her between us and carried her back inside to her room. We cleaned the wound but found the bleeding difficult to stop. We gathered clean cloths and folded them into thick pads taking turns holding them firmly to her head. Eventually the bleeding slowed and after an hour finally ceased. She did not seem to be in pain as she made no sounds at all. She has been asleep since we found her on the shed floor."

"Can you estimate how much blood she might have lost and would one of you please put a large kettle of water on to boil?" I asked. I felt the loss of blood must have not been too great as she continued to sustain good color and, other than not responding, her pulse remained strong. I needed to clean and sterilize the wound and suture it closed.

"Maybe ¼ liter of blood was lost", Evangaline spoke up. "The blood on the ground in the shed and the blood from the soaked pads would indicate perhaps that or a little more."

Significant but not worrisome. What concerned me most was her continued unresponsiveness and the fact that she had now had no water or nourishment for more than 15 hours. Suture first and deal with that after.

I went with Sister Evangaline to the kitchen and scrubbed my hands. Sister Jeanne was taking care of cleaning the bandages they had used and had put a kettle on to boil as I had asked. I poured a portion of the boiling water into another pot setting it back on the stovetop and placing my scissors and needles into the water as it resumed boiling. I asked for a small table to be placed beside the chair in Sister Agnès's room and asked Sister Dominique to scrub her hands as well, as she would assist me.

I wrapped the wet implements in a clean piece of muslin to dry and carried it back to Sister Agnès's room. Henri was standing just outside Sister's bedroom door, his hat still in his hands.

"Henri, do you have a drink stronger than wine in your wagon? One with a very high alcohol content?" I asked.

"I am sure I have something but are you wise to take drink that strong before you begin to sew? Maybe just a little port to calm the nerves Mademoiselle?" he asked.

I couldn't help but smile. "It isn't for me Henri. I need it to sterilize the wound and perhaps provide a little to drink for Sister Agnès if she awakens during the suturing."

He smiled in return and hurried to the wagon. I knew he would come back with what was needed. He always did.

I finished laying out my few implements atop the side table onto the muslin as Henri walked into the room and handed me a small corked stone jug. The jug looked much worn and as I lifted off the cork, what was inside smelled very strong and very old as well.

"What is it?" I asked Henri as I wrinkled my nose.

"I am not altogether sure Marie. It is from a local gentleman from whom I purchase the tonic for other local gentlemen. All of who assure me it is highly medicinal!"

"Yes, it certainly smells like it will clean a wound quite well!" I responded as I threaded my needle tying a secure knot at the end.

Sitting in the chair and holding a small pad of cloth below the cut to catch the alcohol as it flowed into and out of the wound, I patted the wound dry and proceeded to close the gash. Fifteen stitches later and with more alcohol poured into the wound, I let it dry, covered it with lavender salve and a clean bandage of muslin and found myself sending a prayer to *La Vierge Marie* asking that it not become infected. Again, it was all the tending I knew to do. Sister Agnès had not stirred during the time it took to make that straight seam of her flesh and yet I felt there was some sense of awareness on her part. We would let her rest and then we would see what to do next.

I gathered my tools into the muslin and left Sister Evangeline again at the bedside, while the remaining five of us moved into the kitchen. A kettle was put on for tea and we drank and had some bread and honey as we talked through the incident.

Henri soon joined us saying, "I went to the shed and it appears The Good Sister fell against a hatchet. The hatchet was leaned among the assortment of other tools; head side down. The blood spilled has soaked in and dried dark on the ground. The hatchet head is covered with dried blood as well. It is astounding that her injury was not greater; astounding that she is alive."

"It is not her time to be taken from us! Sister Agnès has had some experience with close calls of this sort and we always attribute it to the fact that she has angels of protection," Sister Jeanne chimed in as she refilled our tea cups.

"What other close calls do you mean?" I asked

The Sisters began to recount stories of Sister Agnès's escapes from serious injury; multiple bee stings that would cause her eyes to swell up and breathing to become shallow, days of vomiting from mushrooms she "would try first", measles and other illnesses of unknown origin.

"But no unexplained dizziness, previous falls or injuries to her head?" I inquired.

"No, none," they assured me.

We finished our tea and together went to check on our patient. Her head was cool, pulse and breathing steady. I wanted to see firsthand the site of her accident and Henri accompanied me to the shed to have a look for myself.

The shed was barely light now as it was late afternoon. This wooden outbuilding was old and tilted, long and narrow. Nails studded the wooden support beams along both the left and right walls. From one of the nails on the right wall hung a heavy jute rope, its length extended down the wooden wall with the end tamped into the dirt floor of the shed. I stopped and scuffed at the rope where it ended in the dirt. With my boot, I uncovered a 25" diameter loop partially exposed in the dirt of the floor. This loop was approximately a body length away from the far end of the shed where the tools lay leaned into the corner. The hatchet still lay on the ground where Sister Agnès fell, its thick metal blade indeed, colored with dried blood. Henri and I looked up at each other at the same time.

"I hate ropes." I said quietly.

"Mon Dieu!" he replied while shaking his head. And laying a hand gently on my arm, we turned and walked back toward the convent.

Henri and I shared with the other Sisters our theory that Sister Agnès's shoe had caught in the loop of the rope causing her to fall forward hitting the hatchet blade as she fell to the ground. They all moved as one out to the shed to do as I had done, to see firsthand what may have caused Sister Agnès's injury. That left Henri and I to sit with Agnès.

"Henri," I started, "I want to stay here for the night. It concerns me that Sister has not yet awaken, and I need to exam her closely when she does. She will also need water and whatever food she can take".

"Of course Marie. I will remain as well. The Sisters will be reassured by your presence."

"I will keep the first watch from now till midnight and change off with the other Sisters." I told Henri.

The Sisters had returned from the shed, all agreeing with our conclusion regarding the cause of the fall. All agreed as well that having Henri and I remain with them through the night was wise. We assigned who would take what hours of watch with Sister. I knew these next few hours were crucial and even when the other Sisters encouraged me to get some sleep, I was determined to remain awake and with Sister Agnès at least until midnight.

The Sisters retired to their respective rooms and I settled in for my watch. At his insistence, Henri brought blankets from his wagon and slept on the floor outside Sister's bedroom. By ten o'clock I found myself barely able to keep my eyes open; my head continually falling onto my chest. I began to hum to stay awake and then my fingers began to accompany my humming of "Für Elise", tapping out the notes softly upon Sister Agnès's bed sheets. I found the humming helped keep me awake and I "played" several short pieces using Sister's bed as my keyboard.

Suddenly, after my fourth playing of "Für Elise", Sister Agnès opened her eyes, looked directly at me and said, "I played that piece when I was a girl."

I was so surprised at hearing her voice, I let out a small gasp. She smiled and fell asleep again.

"Sister, Sister," I said as firmly as possible and gently shaking her arm. "You need to stay awake. You need to drink some water and try to eat some food. Sister, please try and open your eyes again!"

She once more opened her eyes, smiled ever so slightly and returned to sleep yet again. At least I knew she could be roused. I was desperate to have her drink some liquid, and as I propped her head I managed to have her take a few sips of water from the cup laid ready on the table. I was relieved when she didn't choke, but swallowed, and in my firm nurse's voice told her she must take some more sips. Again, she was initially compliant, and managed to take more water before turning her head to the side in refusal.

This was encouraging progress, and although I wanted to share this good news with the others, I also didn't want to disturb their sleep. And so I sat back again in my chair and knew when it was my turn to sleep, I could do so with instructions for each bedside Sister to rouse Sister Agnès at least once a shift and insist she drink. In the morning we would make thin cereal in milk with honey and have her eat.

Over the next three days, Sister Agnès had short periods of wakefulness. She was able to drink and eat small amounts with assistance, which I required her to do every three hours throughout the day. She drifted in and out of consciousness, and was not yet able to sit or stand. When she wet her bed sheets I was again encouraged. I instructed the Sisters that they move and bend her arms and legs three times a day, preferably 30 minutes after she had eaten. Her muscles needed to retain some strength as I wanted her on her feet as soon as possible. At the end of the third day she could squeeze my hands more tightly than the day before and verbally answer "yes" and "no".

Henri had gone back to my house on day two bringing back with him my horse and wagon. He fed Pedro and the chickens and assured them I would be home soon. On the fourth day Sister woke with the sun to smile at us and tell us how foolish we all were to worry so about her. Ah, our Sister was still herself.

The wound was healing well with no signs of infection with vital signs remaining normal. Sister was now sitting up at the bedside table long enough to slowly eat her meals and converse for short periods of time with the other Sisters and myself as she gained strength. In my judgment, she had suffered a significant concussion and it would be several weeks or longer before she totally regained use of all her faculties. Based on her reactions and responses, I was confident that she had not suffered a more significant event previous to the fall.

Henri and Donkey took their leave and headed north at the end of day four. I left the morning of the next day, leaving detailed instructions regarding Sister Agnès's care, which included having her begin to take short walks about her room supported by the others. With hugs all around, I assured them I would return in three days, and climbed aboard my wagon and headed for my home. The Sisters were sending me home with jars of our lavender honey, honey cakes made during those days of nursing, fresh loaves of baked bread and a basket full of dried meats and cheeses.

I loved climbing onto my high wagon perch and, giving Horse his head to get us home, I could look out across the land. Here atop my wagon seat, my view was unobstructed, allowing me to take in the sights and smells of each changing season. The early winter air was fresh with lingering dampness upon the ground, the birds that stayed through the seasons were waking, and patches of last color lay scattered across the land.

A seat cushion always sat beneath me as the road was ever bumpy and full of pocks and holes. Horse must have gotten dizzy as he weaved around or between them all. He knew the way so well I held the reins only to keep my balance during the jostling and the weaving. Somehow Horse maintained a steady pace as we made our way - neither fast nor slow.

After an hour of riding, the poplars along the river bank began to take form; their branches now nearly bare. The trees were always lovely to me in any season. The sun was now up a little higher and illuminated all that lay ahead. My breath lay as a mist in front of me and I was becoming more chilled and looked forward to laying fresh fires in my stove.

Almost home, I experienced that morning a joy beyond any I could remember. Visions, smells, and sounds of life wrapped all around enfolding me in cleansing renewal. Tears of relief and thankfulness were wet on my face. I could still feel joy and recognized that this life I was making was the one I desperately wanted. The suffocating paralysis I had known lifted fully, replaced by the knowledge that I still had much to offer and much to receive. The seeds had been planted; seeds of abiding friendship and a renewal of self-worth. I was still a competent nurse. I could even here, even now in this place, tend and heal again. Even more glorious, I had become a part of people's lives, people I cared about deeply and welcomed having them in turn care about me. My heart was full as I looked into the morning's sun and celebrated this new day's beginning and going home to my house in Meuse.

Arriving home, I found a letter had been pushed beneath my front door. Seeing it was from Solange I opened it quickly, and realizing that the letter was written by Papa, the first I had received in his own hand, startled me so that I sat down heavily upon the divan. He was telling me they were quite settled now in New York, and went on to describe a life in which both he and Solange were finding great satisfaction. So much so, that he was insisting that I make plans to travel to New York for a visit in either April or May of this next spring. All of the contentment I had experienced just minutes ago seemed to evaporate as I contemplated what might be Papa's intentions for my planning a visit to America.

Afterword From the Author

When everyone around me was enthralled with all things lavender, extolling its benefits and how the very sight and smell prompted positive feelings of calm and contentment, I was very puzzled. Even a hint of the fragrance from a pretty ribbon-tied bunch of lavender in a quaint shop would find me close to tears with feelings of sadness rolling over and over me.

Yet somehow I was continually drawn to lavender. The purple periwinkle color had always been my favorite and I appreciated the many varieties of the plant itself. Certainly here in the Pacific Northwest lavender graced many a garden. Growing in someone else's garden was fine – just not my own. Tulips and daffodils made me happy, but there was no desire of adding anything lavender to my garden.

During this same time period beginning about 1994, I would wake up in the early morning completely conscious of the fact that I had not been merely dreaming, but was instead experiencing some type of vivid memory. My earliest memory of the stories that comprise this book were of the young soldier named Laurent. I could completely recall the bedroom he slept in, saw the pale yellow curtains fluttering around the open window and was taken over by grief at the loss of him.

This memory of Laurent was recurring and became so familiar that I was eventually able to separate my feelings and begin to pay attention to details and explore the memory. I could easily recall more of this place I saw so clearly in my mind. I was in a house and there were other injured men in this house with me. In my mind I could walk through all the rooms of this house and experience every detail of light, texture and smell. Walking out the back door and through the window at the top of the landing, I could see rolling fields of lavender. Out the front door I could walk down steps crossing the dirt road to the other side and stand alongside a river. I could feel and hear the breeze move through the branches of the poplar trees on the river's bank. It was all familiar. All known to me. It was real.

I didn't share these memories with anyone at that time, but in July of 1995, I had an experience which allowed me to acknowledge that these vivid recollections were ones I wanted to claim as my own and experience in more detail. My sister Kathleen and her husband Doug had been visiting and in attendance at one of our five daughters' wedding the day before, a Saturday. The next day along with my husband Terry, the four of us went on a day trip to Victoria, British Columbia. It was a warm sunny summer's day and we strolled through the side streets looking at the wares of the vendors and artisans commenting again and again on how wonderful the wedding had been, and how great it was to be together now in Victoria.

As we slowly walked along, my eyes caught those of a young woman in her vendor tent. The sign above the tent said "Palm Readings". We smiled at one another and I continued walking with my family. After five minutes or so I turned to my husband Terry and told him I had to go back and see the palm reader. This was a very unusual thing for me to do, as I had never had my palm read and never even had an interest in doing so. However, the pull toward this person was so strong that I handed my husband my jewelry and bag and headed back toward her tent.

The woman's tent was approximately 5' x 5'. She had two chairs facing each other and a small table on which sat some printed material and two round balls of crystal. Each were the size of large oranges. One was pale pink and the other clear with flecks of white and silver gray. She had me sit in one of the folding chairs and asked me to hold the clear ball in both hands. She pulled her chair to the small table never glancing toward me as I held this orb in my hands. After a few minutes she asked if I felt anything. I told her no, I felt nothing. She got up from her chair bringing the pink crystal ball with her and taking the clear one from my hands, she laid the pink ball into my palms. She wasn't back in her chair more than a minute when I told her I was feeling something. The crystal ball was becoming very warm in my hands. Very warm! The feeling was unexpected and disconcerting!

She got up, removed the ball from my palms, placed it on the table, pulled her chair across from mine and told me now she would read both my palms. In one, she said, she saw the past and in the other the present and future.

She proceeded to tell me specific details about my life over the last 20 years. I said little, wanting to neither confirm nor deny anything she said lest I give any hint leading her to think what she was telling me was false or true. What she told me of my life was indeed true, the accuracy of her knowledge quite astonishing. To think a stranger could know these aspects of my past! But that was only the beginning of my surprise.

When she lifted my other palm and began to talk of the present and of my future, her words came fast and, as I wanted to remember everything she said, I had a hard time keeping up with her. She told me I was in a "healing profession" and worked primarily with children. She said I was a teacher and therapist, all of which was and is true. She asked if I ever puzzled over the fact that my work resulted in helping in ways that were sometimes not easily explained. At this point I told her yes; that I felt I often connected with patients, particularly children, on a deep intuitive level that could not always be explained scientifically, or in the context of my training and experience as a speech-language pathologist.

She told me that I brought to this life experiences and training from a past life. She said I was very intuitive and those I taught and worked with knew that I cared deeply for them and they were able to respond openly and with trust.

She then asked if I had knowledge or memories of any past lives. My heart began to race and I was at odds as to how to answer this question. Tears came to my eyes as I realized that those vivid memories I had been having were of patients that I had been caring for in a place very real in another time. She said that she could see I had at least three past lives. I shared with her that the majority of my memories of a previous time were during and after WWI in France.

I left that palm reader feeling shaken to my core. I was also extremely excited, and as I rejoined my family, my only thought was to find a place to sit and write down everything she had told me and to begin to write my memories as well. On the ferry trip back to the U.S., I made hasty notes of all I remembered the palm reader saying and typed it up when we returned home.

The memories continued with greater clarify into events during that long-ago time. People became familiar and memories of who they were, what was said, and events during that time in my life became clearer. Beginning in 2010, I began to write down these memories of the story you have read. The story came to me not in a sequential order, but the middle chapters came first, then followed by the beginning and ending chapters. I wrote them each in whatever order they were remembered. Amazingly, they have flowed into a seamless story of a life I remember living. I have spent the last two years expanding those memories into this book, doing a great deal of research along the way, verifying the historical accuracy of what happened in France during those years surrounding WWI and staying true to the memories of Marie and our shared experiences. This journey of re-membering has been unique and life-changing.

My very best to you,
Gail Marie Noble-Sanderson
2014

Historical Perspective – Battle of Verdun

The high rates of mortality experienced in World War I, due in great part to "advances" in weaponry including long range rifles, machine and turret guns, tanks and lethal chemical gas fired in shells, bombing aircraft and submarines equipped with weaponry, terminated the lives of 10 million people.

The death toll was unexpected and unprecedented. During the Battle of Verdun alone, which began on February 21, 1916 and ended in November or December 1916, the following statistics have been reported by armies, countries and historians:

- 708,777 total French and German soldiers were killed, wounded or missing in battle.
  +305,440 French and Germans soldiers died in battle at Verdun.
  +An additional 403,337 French and Germans soldiers were wounded or missing in the battle.
- One tenth of all French soldiers lost in WWI were lost in the Battle of Verdun.
- Soldiers on the killing fields of Verdun died at a rate of 1 death per minute, round the clock, for the almost 10 months of battle.
- By 1918 there were 630,000 war widows in France.

The original plan to evacuate the wounded from the battlefields such as Verdun by train to hospitals in Paris was short lived due to the carnage inflicted by the weaponry. The soldiers' wounds were often so extensive that any hope of saving their lives meant immediate medical attention, and depended on the efforts and skills of the surgeons and nurses in the field hospitals set up on the periphery of the battle lines.

Two million Frenchmen were dead by the end of the war. The majority of these dead were young men who had served in the infantry. The government continued, after the war, to strongly encourage women to renew their country by resuming their rightful and proper roles as wives and mothers. This was difficult to achieve in light of the fact that so many men were forever lost, and the children the country wanted women to bare were never to be. This Great War, the war to end all wars, left nations depleted, devastated European cultures and, on the souls of the 10 million dead, laid the groundwork for World War II.

References:

Ian Ousby, *The Road to Verdun.* New York: Random House, 2002.

John Keegan, *The First World War. New York: Random House, 1999.*

Historical Perspective – Lavender

Throughout 2500 years of recorded history, including accounts from the Egyptians, Phoenicians, Romans and French, lavender has been used extensively and in a myriad of creative ways. It has been a part of the mummification process, cleansing and healing wounds and aches throughout time and wars, purifying the air, perfuming bodies and homes and as an aphrodisiac. Candles, oils, lotions and ornamentation in the form of wreaths and arrangements of its stems and flowers continue to be consumed worldwide. Culinary lavender provides us with aromatic and medicinal teas, flavors baked goods as well as stimulating our taste buds in salad dressings, cooking oils, sauces and candies. Its uses are only limited by ones imagination.

Due to the many varieties of this hearty plant, cultivation of lavender has long existed in many parts of the world including New Zealand, Australia, and Japan and throughout Europe including England and France. Lavender has been grown in France for centuries, primarily in the region of Provence where the climate of sun and rocky well drained soil of the hills and mountains create the perfect combination for lavender to grow in wild abundance. During the 19th century, the oil of lavender was often collected in portable stills brought into the fields at harvest. Increased demand in the 1920's saw lavender begin to be cultivated more formally as a commercial crop and the harvest was transported to larger permanent stills for processing.

Lavender has a rich and fabled history of positive properties including the ability of its rich aroma to affect us spiritually. Some, like the fabled Lumurians, purposed lavender could transport one to a place of great peace and higher consciousness. Certainly its varietal beauty and fragrance alone cause us to pause and reflect as its presence in our gardens and our homes can stir our memories and, perhaps for you as with me, provide inspiration for a great adventure into the other known.

Historical Perspective – Apiculture and Honey

Like lavender, honey and the gathering of honey from bee combs has been depicted in historical drawings and writings since ancient times. It is estimated there are approximately 20,000 species of wild bees. Hunting and gathering peoples harvested honey from the hives of wild bees found in rocks and trees but in the process securing the honey, the hives and the bees were often destroyed.

Some of the earliest evidence of the domestication of bees appears by the Egyptians (2422 BCE) and the myriad uses for honey have been depicted in the hieroglyphics of ancient tombs and temples across ancient cultures. Honey was used extensively for both pleasure and medicinal purposes often as a healing agent in salves and ointments, in cosmetics and, of course, for the pure enjoyment of eating honey. It was the nectar of Hindu gods, was eaten as part of celebrations and ceremonies by many cultures, is referenced in the writings of early Sumerians, Babylonians, and the honey bee was a symbol of royalty for the ancient Romans.

Beginning in the mid-1770's, the Western Honey Bee (apis mellifera) was domesticated throughout Europe in sustainable hives, made first of straw and evolving into rectangular structures made of cedar, pine, cypress and today sometimes of polystyrene. In 1792 a blind Swiss naturalist and bee keeper, Francois Huber, experimented with "leaf hives" which were made of wooden frames, levered together and opened much as the pages or leafs in a book. This allowed for the study of the nature of bees and greatly increased understanding of their hive building and habits. In the mid-1800's a pastor in Pennsylvania, Lorenzo Langstroth, developed sustainable hives that incorporated what came to be known as "the bee space". This one quarter to three eighths of an inch between the comb frames allowed the bees to move freely and allowed ample room between the combs to keep the frames completely separate one from the other preventing damage to the combs themselves. Sustainable hives developed on the principles set forth by Huber, Lansgstroth, Mehring and other early apiculturist enthusiasts and researchers, greatly enhanced the understanding of all things bees preserving the bee colonies while allowing the honey and wax to be harvested efficiently.

Meanwhile, at about this same time, in the mid-1800's, an Austrian army officer named Francesco de Hruschka, developed the hand-cranked centrifuge which allowed the individual honey combs, several at a time, to be placed inside a glass container and by turning the handle and spinning the honey combs around, the honey was loosened from the combs flowing into the bottom of the centrifuge's container and out through a spout. Viola! The industry of commercialized honey and wax production was born and is very much alive today. It thrives across the world in large enterprises, small cottage industries, within the bounds of cities on rooftops and for anyone who has space enough for a hive or two. Or, as with Marie, placing hives among the hectares of wild lavender.

Many varieties of lavender now grace my home gardens and the summer is filled with their beautiful blossoms alive with bees!

CPSIA information can be obtained at www.ICGtesting.com
Printed in the USA
BVOW03s1812080714

358090BV00001B/2/P